Fallin

CW01665009

Caleb

THE FALLING SERIES #7

Copyright © 2017 by Tracy Lorraine

All rights reserved.

No part of this book may be reproduced in any form or by any electronic or mechanical means, including information storage and retrieval systems, without written permission from the author, except for the use of brief quotations in a book review.

Edited by Pinpoint Editing

Proofread by Sisters Get Lit.erary

Cover design by Sammi Bee Designs

Deanna, for everything you do. x

Chapter 1

Taylor

New Year's Eve two years ago...

If you were to ask me what my perfect man would look like then the man I'm currently staring at across the room would be him. Tall, slim, obviously fit and wrapped in a skinny fit grey suit. Perfectly styled caramel hair with a sharp jawline and full kissable lips—lips that I could kiss for hours. I lose myself in my imagination as I stare at his mouth.

I have no idea who this guy is but my gaydar is telling me that it's game on. That plus the fact I know he's aware of my attention. He may be stood next to a stunning curvy blonde but I can tell from here he's not interested in her. From what I can tell he's trying to look like he is but his eyes keep flicking over to me every so often. Each time our eyes connect I can't help the butterflies that erupt in my stomach.

I want to spend the night with this man.

If I'm honest I think I could spend the rest of my life looking at this man, he's perfect. And trust me, that isn't something I say lightly. I've vowed to never have forever with anyone.

After another glance back at me I watch him place his hand on the small of the woman's back as he whispers something in her ear. She looks up at him and smiles. I see that she's almost as stunning as him when I catch a glimpse of her face. She's pretty fuckable. Not in the way he is though. She could warm my bed for a night and I wouldn't think twice about her after she leaves. Him though. Fuck me, I want him.

I watch as he walks toward the toilet but finding the door locked he changes direction and heads out of the room.

I stay where I am for a minute before following. Lilly is distracted talking to her sister so I slip away unnoticed. Spending my New Year's Eve with my best friend and her family isn't exactly what I had in mind for tonight but when she told me her boyfriend had bailed on her I couldn't say no to her sad little face. I'm hoping this evening may just be looking up now though.

When I get out to the hallway I look at the two sets of stairs. Knowing there is only a bedroom and en suite downstairs, I opt for heading to the top floor. After opening a couple of doors and finding only bedrooms I put my hand onto the handle of the final door up here. Slowly I push it down but to my disappointment the door doesn't open. I know he's inside though.

I stand back against the wall and wait.

After watching this guy for the last couple of hours my patience is wearing a little thin but the memory of those lips remind me that I'd probably wait forever to get a taste of him.

After a minute I hear the toilet flush and then the tap run. My excitement builds as I wait for him to appear. It's like time slows down as I hear the lock being turned and then the door being pulled open.

I take a deep breath and wait.

"I knew it was you," he says after a couple of seconds. "I was hoping you might follow me."

The knowledge that he came up here on purpose seriously excites me. "Why's that?"

"Because you've been eye-fucking me for the last two hours and it's driving me crazy." He says so seriously that I have no idea if I've pissed him off or if he liked it. He slowly takes a step toward me before continuing with what he was saying. "I don't think anyone has ever managed to turn me on quite so much from the other side of the room."

I let out the breath I was holding as his words settle in my brain. It's obvious he's a little drunk but I don't think he's had enough to not know what he's doing right now.

"So what do you say, stranger?" he says as he steps right up in front of me.

"I say fuck yes," I announce before bringing my hand up to the back of his head and pull his lips to mine.

Although he was obviously keen it takes a second for him to react to me. It's only a second though before his lips open for me and I feel his weight pressing me back into the wall.

I was right. Those lips can kiss.

Present…

"Taylor, we're here," I hear somewhere in the distance.

I feel warmth across my cheek a second before his scent fills my nose. I'd know it's him anywhere. It's like his body talks to mine.

I feel a pull across my chest and it hurts like fuck. I suck in a breath as the pressure goes away. Memories of this afternoon slam into me and I go to open my eyes, only they won't open. Not more than a millimetre or two.

"Shit, sorry. Come on, we're here."

His face is still right in front of mine but his usual carefree look is long gone. Instead he looks stressed and worried. Is it awful of me to feel ecstatic that he looks that way because of me? It's nice to know he does care. He puts so much effort into trying to be unaffected by me but I know it's all an act. It's why I haven't ever given up on him.

I feel his hands come under my armpits as he pulls me up from the seat. He manages to manhandle me out of the car and my jelly-like legs just about hold me up. Together we stumble toward the front door. I've only seen pictures of this house but it's even more impressive in real life. When I visited Lilly after she moved to Devon, her and Lucas were still living in his hotel. They only moved in here a few weeks ago. I've been desperate to see what she's done with the place but I wasn't expecting my first visit to be quite like this.

I feel my body giving up on me as I stand at the front

door clinging on the best I can to Caleb. I need to lie down. I need to sleep. Fuck, I need more painkillers.

When the door gets pulled back I just about make out Lucas with Lilly hanging over his shoulder. One look at his guests though and he drops her to her feet.

"Shit, what happened?" he asks seconds before Lilly turns toward us.

"Shit, Taylor. What happened to him?" she asks Caleb as I feel Lucas grab on to my other side. He's just in time because I was about to hit the floor.

They both start to move me into the house but blackness starts to descend on me so I struggle to focus on what they are saying.

"I know you," I hear Lilly say to Caleb as I feel myself get lowered on to what I hope is the sofa. "But I can't place you."

"I'm Caleb, Beth's brother. Taylor lives with me." Lilly doesn't know anything about Caleb, other than he's Beth's brother, because I haven't told her about him. It's killed me to do so and I don't really know why I've kept it from her but I have. Maybe it's because I want him so badly but he won't allow it. Maybe it's because I've fallen for him and yet I've barely touched him. I'm sure I could come up with loads of reasons if I thought about it.

"Oh, it's you," Lilly says as if she's just figured out some impossible puzzle. I know she's known there's been something going on with me but she's never come out and asked which I'm grateful for. "What happened?" she asks again but I don't hear Caleb's response. I drift off into the blackness where the pain disappears and I can put what happened to one side knowing I'm with my real family. Lilly is my family, she has been for a few years now. Unlike my blood relations I know I can rely on her and I know she'll look after me. Caleb would have been great but he doesn't understand, not yet anyway. Lilly on the other hand knows everything.

Caleb

I've been away on an amazing shoot for the last two days and I'm buzzing to tell someone about it. Hoping that Taylor will be home from work I jog up the stairs to our flat with my overnight bag over my shoulder.

I don't think anything of it when I find the door ajar. Taylor is pretty useless like that. Clearly me moaning about him leaving it open last time fell on deaf ears.

"Taylor, the fucking door's open again." I may have moved to a nicer building but we are still in the middle of London. Fuck knows who we're sharing this building with. But he's happy to leave the door swinging open for anyone to stroll in. If he's left it open because he's too busy fucking someone while I was away I'm going to be seriously pissed off.

"Taylor," I shout again when I get no response. This time I do hear something but it's not so much a response as a groan. I head toward the kitchen where it sounded like it came from but before I find him I find blood.

"Fuck, Taylor," I say to myself as I pick up my pace.

"Fuck," I repeat when I find him curled up in the corner of the kitchen covered in blood.

I crouch down next to him to inspect the damage but there is too much blood to really see anything.

"I'm ringing an ambulance."

"No, please. No."

"Taylor, you're in a right state. You need to be looked at."

"I'm... fine. Please," he begs. "Lilly."

"What?"

"Take me... to... Lilly... please."

"Taylor, she lives in Devon. It's hours away. You need to go to A&E not fucking Devon."

"No," he says again with much more determination behind it. He manages to uncurl himself enough so he can sit up a little and look at me.

The state of his face makes me suck in a breath. I've known for a long time that my feelings for this guy are too strong but I've managed to lock them down. Taylor's a player and I've had my fill of those over the years. He may tell me he's changed but a leopard never changes his spots.

I fight the urge I have to wrap myself around him and never let go. Instead I stand up and pull my phone out of my pocket to call for an ambulance. Fuck knows what he might have broken. I shouldn't be moving him.

"Caleb. Please," he begs again while staring into my eyes. His dark ones into my blue. "Take me to Lilly. I need her."

"Fuck's sake, Taylor."

"Please."

"Fine. Let's clean you up a bit first." I say caving to the pathetic look he's giving me. I can only say no to him so many times.

New Year's Eve two years ago...

I clock him the minute he walks in. He arrived with a pretty little blonde though so at first I think my luck is out. That's until he starts looking my way. He looks too good to be true. Tall, dark and fucking gorgeous. His dark, almost black, hair is shaved close to his head. His eyes are the same colour and his stare is intense. One look from him touches me deep, I've never experienced that before. His skin is tanned and covering the most incredibly muscular frame. My mouth waters for a taste.

I know he's interested so I come up with a way to hopefully get him alone. I've never made it a secret that I'm gay but I've never openly told anyone other than my sister, Beth, and my old school friend, Abbi. I'm pretty sure everyone knows though, well apart from my mother who dreams of weddings, big hats and babies. I've never had the heart to ruin them by telling her the truth. It doesn't mean I won't. I've just never found anyone important enough to introduce to them. I want that to change though. I'm done bed-hopping. I want to find someone I can share my life with. I want fun inside and outside of the bedroom. Someone I can trust to be faithful.

I watch as one of the partygoers takes themselves to the bathroom on this floor of Molly and Ryan's house and I use that as an opportunity to leave the room in favour of the bathroom upstairs after making a show of trying the locked door. I glance his way as I leave the room and just as I hope, he's watching my every move.

When I hear the door handle being wiggled I suddenly feel a bolt of nerves hit me. I haven't been with anyone since I decided to stop pissing about. I haven't found anyone that's interested in anything more than a quick shag. I'm hoping this guy is going to be different. My gut says that he's different.

I swallow down my nerves, unlock the door and step out. Those nerves soon disappear when I look into his dark, hungry eyes. I stand still and let his eyes run over me. It allows me time to do the same to him. His crisp white shirt is pulled tight across his broad shoulders and shows off his sculpted chest and slim waist perfectly. His pants are tight and I desperately want to ask him to turn around so I can check out his ass.

I don't know what comes over me in those few minutes. I think it's the effect of his dark eyes but after a few words I step right up to him, our lips collide and I run my tongue along his bottom lip. When I feel his sneak out to play with mine I lose strength in my legs and have to lean into him to keep myself up.

His fingers grip on to the short hair at the back of my head and he tilts it to the side slightly so we can deepen the kiss.

His lips are like a fucking drug. From the second mine touched them I know I never want to give them up.

But just like my thoughts earlier he soon proves to me that he is indeed too good to be true.

"You're coming home with me tonight."

His words are like a bucket of cold water. I take a big step back and look at him. He's perfect in every way, except just like all the others, all he wants is a fuck.

"No, I'm not."

His eye's crinkle at the sides as he thinks about what I just said.

"I'm sorry, then what's all this about?"

"This isn't just about a quick fuck. I'm looking for more. So unless you can offer the possibility of more, then I'm not interested." It's so hard to stay strong because every part of me other than my brain is screaming at me to take him up on his offer. Especially my cock, that's currently trying to break free of my pants to get to him.

"You're fucking kidding?" he asks with a laugh.

"No, I'm not." Those words make his smile falter a little.

"So you lured me up here for nothing?"

"No, I was hoping you'd be different. I'm not going to go into this pretending I want something I don't. I'm done with one-night stands. I want something more and I was hoping being honest about that wouldn't scare you off. But clearly it has."

"I don't do more,*" he admits. "I'm pretty sure if I were to ever change my mind though it could be for you."*

His admission shocks and excites me but it's not enough to forget what I'm looking for.

He suddenly steps forward. His hand slips inside my jacket and runs down my side. He squeezes it into my pocket and grabs my phone, not before gently stroking my cock with his finger causing me to suck air into my lungs.

His touch makes me dizzy and it's almost enough to say 'fuck it let's go'.

"What're you doing?" I ask as he unlocks my cell and starts tapping at the screen. Seconds later I hear his ring.

"Just in case you change your mind and a quick but amazing fuck is just what you need."

I open my mouth to tell him that won't be happening but he's already striding off down the hallway.

I look down at my cell that he placed back in my hand.

Taylor.

I stare at his name on my phone for a few seconds. It scares the shit out of me when it vibrates in my hand.

Taylor: Ring me anytime, stranger. x

What the fuck just happened? I ask myself as I make my way back to the party.

Present...

"What happened?" Lilly asks again, pulling me from my thoughts.

"I've no idea. I found him like this in our kitchen. He's refused to tell me. Just kept saying he wanted you."

"Why didn't you take him to a hospital? That'd probably be more useful."

"I fucking tried but he made me promise not to. You know Taylor better than anyone so I know you understand how hard it is to say no to him."

"Yes, I know," Lilly mutters in understanding.

"Shall we get him upstairs?" Lucas asks over Lilly's shoulder.

The three of us look down at his passed out broken body in silence.

"Are you sure nothing's broken that needs medical attention?" Lilly asks.

"I don't think so. Maybe a rib or two but not much can be done about that anyway."

"Let's get him upstairs, we can assess the damage in the morning," Lucas decides as he steps toward the sofa.

With Lucas on one side and me on the other we just about manage to get Taylor up the stairs and into their guest bedroom. Lilly trails behind us with Taylor's shoes that she pulled off when he crashed out on the sofa.

"I'll go get some stuff to clean him up with," she says once we have him on the bed and disappears behind Lucas.

"What the hell happened, Taylor?" I ask knowing I won't get a response. He's out cold. "If this is some sick way of trying to make me admit my feelings then it's not fucking funny." It's been over two years since I met him at Ryan's house but it hasn't lessened my attraction to him. If anything it's only got worse. I knew letting him move in with me was a bad idea.

Chapter 2

Caleb

Lilly reappears a few minutes later with a bag of cotton wool, some warm water and some butterfly sutures. Together we clean him up properly and close the cuts on his eyebrows and lip. I did a pretty rush job at our place.

"You seriously have no idea who did this?" Lilly asks, but I think there's more behind her question.

"Why?" I ask sceptically. "Do you?"

"I have a good idea."

"And," I prompt.

"Not my story to tell. I might be wrong, and I hope I am, but if he wants you to know then he'll have to tell you himself. I'm sorry, Caleb. Thank you for looking after him," she adds when she sees the look on my face.

"What else was I meant to do?"

"You mean a lot to him, you know."

"You didn't even know I existed."

"I didn't know who you were but I've known there's been someone for a long time. Taylor's been... different. I pinpointed it to Christmas two years ago but it's all starting to make sense now. You were at Molly and Ryan's New Year's party, weren't you?"

"Yes."

"You met Taylor that night. He's been weird since then. I think you left a mark."

I shrug my shoulders at her. "I don't know about that," I admit.

"You have. I've never known anyone to make an impact on him. But you have."

Silence descends around us as I think about what she's just said. Taylor's been chasing me for two years, but it's just for that quick fuck I turned him down on, right?

"I'll leave you to it. Call us if you need anything. Our bedroom is down the hall. The other guest room is across the corridor, if you want it. Goodnight, Caleb," she says before giving Taylor a kiss on the forehead and gently running her hand over his hair.

Lilly and I had already removed Taylor's shirt so I set about taking his jeans off so he can sleep comfortably. I undo his belt but I stop when my fingers are hovering above his fly. I told myself I would never get inside Taylor's pants. I look up to his swollen face. He's fast asleep with his long dark eyelashes resting against his bruised cheeks. I feel some of the strength behind that promise I made to myself waning. Even swollen and bruised he's gorgeous. There are times I've nearly caved to him, especially in the early days but I've stayed true to myself. It's got easier, I guess. The longer I've gone without the less I seem to think about it. He affects me no less though when he insists on walking around the flat in only his boxers, or leaves the bathroom door open when he's showering. I'm sure my refusal to sleep with him is now just a game to him.

Two years ago...

"Hey, stranger," I say when I answer the phone.

"Hey. I got bored of waiting for your call."

"You'd have been waiting a long time."

"You've no idea what you're missing out on." Just the sound of his deep voice over the phone makes me think that could very well be true. "Anyway," he says, changing the subject. "A little birdie told me that you've landed yourself a job in London. Congrats, man."

"Uh... thanks," I say with some hesitation. This phone call is weird. I've met this guy once and he's called me to say well done on my new job. There's got to be more to this.

"I was wondering if you wanted to go out and celebrate. There're some insane gay bars in London. I wasn't sure if you'd had time to try any out yet so I thought I'd offer my services."

"You mean you want to get me drunk."

"Well, yeah, that too."

"I'm good, thanks, Taylor."

"Oh come on. You can't tell me that you already have friends in London, you've only been there a few weeks."

"Well..."

"Exactly. This weekend, yeah? I've got it all planned. Soho, Camden—"

"Right, yeah, okay," I say, caving to him. I don't want to admit he's right but he is. My flat is still full of boxes where I've been so busy. I definitely haven't had time to find any possible friends.

Moving to London after returning to England with my family last year from America was always the plan. I dreamt of landing a great job to move down here for but I wasn't against working any job I could find just so I'd hopefully be in the right place at the right time with the agencies to get the job I wanted.

Moving here on my own with no friends or contacts didn't really faze me. Moving across the world as a teenager then not really fitting in anywhere made it less daunting.

I'd never intended on being a model, I wanted a very different kind of job but when I got discovered while I was at college I found out that it really helped with the money side of things. Not only that, it was great fun. I was travelling to all sorts of places, meeting loads of new people, people who I actually fitted in with and could have a conversation with. That was a bit of a novelty after being the misfit Brit for so many years.

I never in a million years thought the one agency I really wanted to work for would even get in contact after I sent them my details but they did. So I found the first available apartment I could and hightailed it down here to get started. The apartment looked pretty grotty online but I was about to live my dream so I rationalised that I could find something better once I was more familiar with the place. What looked grotty online was a proper shithole in real life. But for now it's home and I'll make the best of it.

I run up the stairs to my apartment knowing that Taylor's going to be here any minute. This afternoon's shoot over ran thanks to the airhead I was modelling with. I'm pretty sure she was drunk, or high, or both, actually.

"Shit, fuck's sake," I curse as I try to get my front door open. The lock is sticky and it takes a certain amount of skill to get it to open. Finally I manage it, slam the door behind me and start to strip out of my hoodie and jeans en route to the bathroom. I make the best of the pathetic dribble of water that drips from the pipe sticking out of the wall and wash that woman's scent off me, although it was so strong I'm sure it'll linger around for a few days.

I just pull on a pair of boxer briefs as I hear my front door being knocked. "Fuck," I complain as I grab a shirt and shove my arms through it.

"Whoa, I knew this was a good idea," Taylor says with a beaming smile as I pull the front door open. His eyes run the length of me twice before eventually finding my eyes. His look darker and more intense than I remember. I try to fight the zing of excitement that rushes through me but I can't. "Fuck going out, lets have ourselves a party here."

"Come in," I mutter as I stand back to allow him to enter as I start to do up my buttons.

"Aw, you're ruining it," he complains when he looks back at me.

"You're here to introduce me to some clubs. That's

it." The look of disappointment on his face almost makes me change my mind, but I don't. I'm standing firm by my decision to find someone for more than the night. I want something meaningful. Not just wham, bam, thank you ma'am—or sir to be more precise. "Let me finish getting ready. There's some beer in the fridge," I say over my shoulder as I head to the wardrobe. This studio apartment might be a shithole but thankfully it's big enough to have defined living and sleeping areas even if they are all in one room. And unlike many others I looked at there's just enough space for a bed and a sofa. Bonus.

"Don't take this the wrong way," I hear Taylor say as he heads to the kitchen. I'm not entirely sure it can actually be described as a kitchen though, it's so small you can't really prepare any food in it. Not that I ever cook mind you. "But this place is a bit of a dump."

"I'm well aware," I say with a laugh. "I only saw it online before moving here. I just wanted somewhere cheap for now. Once I get settled here I'll look for somewhere better."

"That won't be hard," I hear him comment.

I finish off getting ready and leave Taylor to whatever it is he's doing. I'm aware that we need to get out of here as soon as possible. Being alone with him in a small and confined space will do nothing for my will power. I hoped he'd turn up and have got really fat and ugly since I last saw him. Not the case though, I think he's hotter than I remember actually.

"Caleb West," I hear him announce from the sofa.

"Yeah?"

"Caleb," he repeats, making me turn around to look at him.

He's not looking up at me like I expected though he's staring down at the coffee table.

"Shit," I mutter to myself because in my rush I forgot to put my photographs away.

"You're an underwear model?" Taylor asks but it's obvious he doesn't need an answer. "Of course you fucking are. You're too fucking hot not to make use of it, I guess."

I feel heat rush to my face. I'm not shy or easily embarrassed but here I am trying my very best not to fall into bed with this guy, who has made it very clear that those are his intentions. I didn't want him looking at me practically naked. It was bad enough I was barely dressed when I answered the door.

"I knew you were familiar to me somehow," he continues, thankfully without looking up to see my humiliation. "I never would have thought it was from a magazine though, or from when I went underwear shopping," he says as he pulls the waistband of his boxers out from behind his shirt showing me they are the same brand as I'm modelling in the photograph he's holding. "I'm practically wearing your underwear. That's pretty hot, right?"

I rush over and scoop up all the photographs before snatching the one he has in his hand away from him. It slips from my fingers and flutters down to the floor landing face down.

"Hey," he complains. "I was looking at that." I watch as he reaches out to grab it but instead of turning it over to

get another look he focuses his attention on the back, at the sticker of the company who took the shots. I don't think anything of it and have another more successful go at taking it away from him.

Taylor takes me to a club that I never would have found by myself and it's just my kind of place—and that's not just because it's filled with hot men. It's got this easy-going, chilled out vibe going on. I can see myself spending a lot of time here from now on.

"Come and dance with me?" Taylor asks for the thousandth time since we arrived. We're on the top level of the club looking down over the dance floor below. I'm kinda transfixed watching all the guys and girls below grinding against each other. It's way more erotic that I thought it would be. Which is exactly why I keep refusing to dance with him. I do not need his body rubbing up against mine. That along with the shots we've had will lead me down a road I don't want to go down with him.

He's hot and seriously my type, there's no denying that. And we click. We click in a way that I've never experienced with another guy before. It makes me think stupid things like he could be the one I'm looking for. It's stupid because he's not interested in relationships. He made that clear the first time I met him and he's made enough comments tonight to confirm that's still the case for him.

I won't risk jumping into bed with him. I don't want to fall back into my old life where my apartment may as well have a revolving door on it. I want more. I think about how happy my sister was in a relationship, well until it all went to shit that is. But I want that. I want to know that I'm going home to someone who is waiting for me. Someone to watch old films with, to go out for meals with. I'm fed up of having to do all that stuff alone after whoever I might have just had a roll around in my bed with has left. It may have taken me a few years to realise it but that life of easy sex doesn't make me happy. I've come to realise that I'd rather go without in the hope that the next man I sleep with could stick around for a while at least.

"For fuck's sake," Taylor declares before I feel him grab my hand and tug. There's no point in me fighting because he's a lot bigger and stronger than me so I allow myself to be pulled along behind him until we are in the middle of the dance floor surrounded by hot, sweaty bodies.

"What's wrong? Don't you think you'll be able to say no this time?" he asks suggestively in my ear as he pulls me to him.

"Uh..."

I allow myself to get carried away. The feel of his hard body up against mine pushes all my earlier thoughts out of my head and I move in time with him to the music. His hands roam all over me and after a while I find that mine are doing the same. Discovering his body, learning that he is a piece of artwork under his clothing. A piece of artwork that I desperately want to appreciate with my eyes as well as my hands.

I wake up to the feeling of someone playing the drums against my skull. My mouth is dry and tastes disgusting, and my stomach feels a little delicate. I stay still for a while trying to remember last night. The last thing I remember was dancing with Taylor.

Taylor!

I sit up way too fast for my hungover head to deal with as I look at the other side of the bed. But it's empty.

Thank fuck.

I hear a snore and I look up to see a body on the sofa. The sunlight from the small window at the other side of the room lights up his body giving me an incredible sight to wake up to. He's covered from the waist down in a blanket but his stomach and chest are all there for the taking. Every perfect tanned inch of skin. Every line and indent all on display for my eyes to follow.

"How're you feeling?"

I'm so lost in his body that his voice scares the shit out of me. I squeal like a little girl and jump up from the bed in fright.

"Jesus, Taylor," I say between pants.

"Sorry," he says as he swings his legs off the side of the sofa and sits up. "How are you feeling? You were out of it."

"Rough. I don't remember drinking that much though," I say as I run through what I can remember of the night before in my head.

"I didn't think so either. You're either an epic lightweight or your drink was spiked."

"How did we get back here?" I ask, hoping to fill in some of the blanks.

"Well, when you started to look a little worse for wear I suggested leaving. You passed out in the taxi and I had to carry you up here."

"Then take my clothes off?" I ask slightly amused.

"It was a tough job but I thought it was for the best."

"Right," I mutter as I begin to make my way to the bathroom in the hope of making myself feel a little more human.

When I return after having a shower I feel a little more alive. I head straight for the kitchen to make some much needed coffee.

"Coffee?" I ask over my shoulder to Taylor who was still sat on the sofa when I walked past looking down at his phone.

"Sure."

I look over my shoulder because the sound of his voice comes from a different place than the sofa.

"For fuck's sake, Taylor," I complain when I see him stood in the middle of the room stretching his arms over his head with a massive hard-on tenting his boxers.

"What?" he asks innocently. "I can't help it, as I'm sure you well know."

"Whatever," I mutter, turning back around to focus on what I should be doing. "Just cover it up," before I do something I shouldn't be doing with it, *I think as I grab the jar of coffee on the side.*

"You know you want it," I hear him say before he disappears into the bathroom.

I lean forward and place my palms on the work surface as I try to get my head straight.

I don't want him. I want something meaningful, *I say*

to myself as a reminder.

Taylor

Present...

My body feels like lead when I wake up. I try to move an arm but it doesn't cooperate.

What the fuck?

I go to open my eyes but they only open halfway and refuse to go any further.

What the fuck?

And then it hits me. Almost with the same force he did.

Fuck.

My eyes begin to focus in the dark room and I see that I'm not alone. Propped up on the headboard on the other side of the bed is a stunningly topless Caleb. Well, if anything can make this better it's the sight of him half dressed. *If only he was totally undressed*, I think to myself as I run my eyes over his sculpted torso.

I look up to see his head resting back against the headboard. His eyes are closed causing his long lashes to rest on his cheekbones and his full lips are slightly parted.

How is it still possible that I still want him as much as I did that first night? I thought I would've got over my infatuation by now. I want to say that the only reason I'm still interested is because he constantly turns me down but I know that's not true. It's not just about sex. It's about him. It's about us.

We just work together. We click in a way I've never discovered with anyone else. I hoped that when I moved in with him last year that he would have some really irritating habit that would turn me off but unfortunately all I discovered by living with him is that he's perfect. I mean, yeah, I find his worn socks on the coffee table after he takes them off while watching TV and he never washes the hair away after shaving but it's his flat he can do what he wants. I'm just crashing the party.

I should have moved out a long time ago. I'm earning enough to get a small place to myself now but something keeps stopping me from mentioning it. He's never brought it up either and I like to imagine that's because he secretly doesn't want me to leave.

It used to freak me out when thoughts of him being *the one* entered my head. You know the one everyone is looking for. The one person who completes you. The one person I never had any intention of looking for let alone finding. But I'm starting to get used to the idea that he could be a constant in my life and it wouldn't worry me. It would far from worry me. I'd love it.

I never thought I would even consider something like that. After years of watching how my mum's *the one* treated her—and me—I knew it wasn't something I wanted. But I'm beginning to realise that what they have isn't the norm. People do actually have loving relationships that work, that make both people happy. Just look at Lilly and Lucas. I thought that was a disaster waiting to happen at the beginning but I've never seen Lilly as happy as she is now. Maybe I could have that.

I pull myself out of my own head and once again

focus on the body in front of me, and that I don't seem to be in a hospital. I smile as I think about the fact he listened to me but I suck in a sharp breath as I feel the skin on my lips crack open.

Caleb instantly sits forward and looks down on me. I can see the worry etched into his face as his eyes focus.

"Are you okay?" he asks, in a panic.

"Yeah. You looked after me," I state.

"Well who else was going to?"

"Hmmm," that is a good question. I've been so wrapped up in work that other than the odd hook-up, and I really mean odd hook-up, my only friend in London is Caleb. Yes my colleagues are great but they're not really my kind of people, not to hang out with regularly anyway.

"What happened, Tay?"

I look into Caleb's concerned eyes and fight the need to lie about what happened. I'm just about to make something up about getting jumped on the way home when there's a light knock at the door.

"Come in," Caleb calls and in a second Lilly's smiling face appears around the door.

"I heard voices, I wanted to come and check on you. You've been asleep for almost thirty-six hours!"

"I'm okay," I say as I attempt to pull myself up to a sitting position. I just about get my arms under me before Caleb starts to help. Fuck I feel useless. He really did a number on me. How I don't have anything broken is beyond me.

Lilly walks over and squeezes her skinny arse on the

bed next to me. She leans forward and gives me a very gentle hug followed by a kiss to the forehead.

"It was *him*, wasn't it?"

"Lilly," I warn but it's pointless because I know she won't stop until she knows the truth.

"Don't *Lilly* me, Taylor."

"Yes, it was him."

"Who's him?" Caleb asks from next to me but neither Lilly or I respond.

"Why? What was his excuse this time?"

"I was trying to help her, Lilly. I thought she meant it this time, I thought she was going to leave him for real. She rang me a couple of weeks ago after he'd gone to the pub. She was a state, I can only imagine what she looked like. She told me it was the final straw this time, that she was leaving. I told her I'd help in any way I could to get her away from that monster. So I booked her a train ticket to come to London. The train should have arrived yesterday afternoon," I admit sadly.

"What happened?"

"He found the ticket. I don't know how. I'd set her up a new email and I was the only other person with the details but somehow he must have found out. I told her I'd meet her at the station and I was going to put her up in a hotel for a few days. As I went to leave I found him stood at the other side of the front door. He was on me before I even knew what was happening. He was spouting all the usual shit about how all I ever did was get in the way, that my dad should have taken me with him when he disappeared. You know how it goes," I say with a shrug because Lilly knows all this so I have no intention of going over it again.

His words haunt me. I'd hoped that as I turned into an adult they wouldn't cut me quite as deep as they did when I was a child but nothing's changed and everything's my fault. It was always my fault that he beat Mum up, it was my fault he lost his job, the list goes on. It's exactly why I got out of there as soon as I could. Mum may be too weak to leave but I certainly wasn't. Although it killed me knowing I was leaving her there.

Over the years I've given her mobile phones so she could contact me if she needed to but I either haven't heard anything or I've discovered via his fists that they'd been discovered.

"Do you think she was actually going to go through with it this time?" Lilly asks.

"I guess we'll never know now. I dread to think what he did to her when he found out."

"Taylor, I know it sounds awful but you need to stop getting involved and trying to help. If she truly wants to leave she's going to have to do it herself, if you force it she'll only go running back to him."

I know all this stuff. I've said the same thing myself over the years. "But she's my mum," I say sadly.

I'd forgotten that Caleb was next to me because he hadn't spoken a word since I started telling Lilly what had happened. But the sound of him letting out a long breath reminds me that he's there.

I feel the warmth of his hand on my shoulder before he says, "your stepdad did this to you?"

I nod once. He doesn't need any more than that, he just heard everything loud and clear.

"And he's done it before?"

"A lot," Lilly answers for me.

Chapter 3

Taylor

"I'm going to leave you two to it," Lilly says when she finishes the coffee she brought up for both of us about thirty minutes ago. Lucas may be in charge of the twins but I can see Lilly twitch every time the sound of their cries carry up here.

"Thank you," I say. "For taking me in."

"Always," she says before disappearing behind the closed door.

"Why didn't you tell me any of that?"

"Why would I? It's not like I enjoy talking about it."

"I get that but you could have told me. I could've helped."

"How?" I ask.

"No idea. But I'd be willing."

"You shouldn't be. No one needs to get in the middle of this. He did this to me," I say pointing at myself, "Someone he brought up almost as if I was his own child. I can't even imagine what he might do to someone he doesn't know."

"I'm so sorry, Tay."

"What for? None of this is your fault. I should be

thanking you. You looked after me, brought me here when I demanded you do so."

"Of course," he says but I'm distracted from his eyes when I feel his hand touch mine.

When I look back up his expression has changed. His eyes are darker and he's biting down on his bottom lip. A bolt of electricity rushes through my aching body and suddenly my bruising is long forgotten.

"Caleb?" I question but it's the wrong thing to do because he blinks at hearing his name and moves away from me. "I need to shower," I say in an attempt not to make a big deal out of whatever just happened.

Caleb moves so he's sat on the edge of the bed with his back to me. He puts his head down in his hands and lets out a huge sigh. I roll over onto my side and place my hand on his back.

"What's wrong?"

"You. You're what's wrong. You have this ability to mess with my head."

Thankfully he's facing away from me so he can't see the shit-eating grin that spreads across my face at his admission.

"Is that so," I say as I run my hand slowly down his back. I don't miss the goosebumps that prick his skin before he jumps up and away from me.

He turns slightly as he heads toward the bathroom and my eyes lock on to his tented jogging bottoms, my smile widens again.

He manages to play it so cool almost 100% of the time but there are these little moments where he allows me to see what it is he really wants but is too scared to admit.

When Caleb re-emerges from the bathroom he seems to have himself in check a little. It's my turn now to be sitting on the edge of the bed which I'm grateful for because it means I get a chance to have a good look at him.

The waistband of his boxers sits well above the low hanging waistband of his jogging bottoms. His chest is perfectly smooth and tanned with muscles and lines in all the right places. I run my eyes up over his chest until I reach his face. His hair is flopping forward over his forehead. It brings back memories of when I found him half dressed before going out in London. He grabs his t-shirt from the chair in the corner of the room but looks up at me before putting it on.

His stare is intense as he looks at me. I don't get a chance to try to figure it out though because he speaks.

"Do you need help... you know... getting to the shower?"

I ache like a bitch but I'm sure I'll be fine. A little bit of help might be nice though.

"That would be good, thank you."

I watch as he drops his t-shirt back to the chair before walking toward me. I make trying to stand up look harder than it actually is and lean on him a little more than I need to as we walk slowly toward the en suite.

I let go of Caleb once we're in the bathroom before stepping away from him and dropping my boxers. I can't help but laugh to myself when I hear him clear his throat behind me.

I muster up as much energy as I can and turn around. I can see him fighting to keep his eyes on my face. It's amusing as hell but after a few seconds he loses the fight and his eyes drop.

"I—" he starts but continues staring.

I take a few steps backwards until I'm in the shower and reach behind me to turn it on. By this time Caleb has regained his composure and is backing up toward the door.

"You're welcome to join me," I offer just as he's about to run.

"Don't," he warns. "Don't tempt me," he says quieter and I can only assume it was a volume he wasn't expecting me to hear over the water. I heard it though. Loud and clear.

I make quick work of the shower and in no time at all I'm hobbling my way out of the bathroom with a towel wrapped around my waist. Much to my disappointment the room is empty.

I find the bag Caleb packed in the middle of the bed. I sit down next to it and pull out some fresh clothes. The second the smell of bacon hits my nose though I throw the clothes on as fast as my body will allow and I head out of the room in search of fried food. After sleeping for hours I'm fucking starving.

I come to a stop just out of sight by the kitchen doorway. Lilly and Caleb are both sat at the table in the centre of the room with steaming mugs in their hands.

"Look," Lilly starts, "tell me to mind my own business but you like him, don't you? What's stopping you? Taylor is besotted with you, he has been for a long time now."

"He's a whore who's only interested in one thing," Caleb says. Hearing him say it out loud hurts. I think I'd rather take a beating from that arsehole again than hear Caleb give his excuses for why he keeps himself at a distance. I'm not stupid, I knew the reason for his constant knock backs but he's never been quite so blunt to my face.

"Yes, he was when we lived together but that was then. I can only go on what he tells me but I get the impression that's changed since moving to London."

"He has his moments," Caleb says more light-heartedly.

"I'm sure he does but doesn't everyone. Surely you haven't been celibate," Caleb doesn't respond but his gaze suddenly becomes very fixated on the table. My heart thuds in my chest as the thought of him being with someone else settles into me. I really fucking hate how it feels. I'd never really thought about what he's been up to. He's never brought anyone back to the flat but then he's away a lot and I have no idea what he's doing then. I guess I just presumed that because he keeps spouting the meaningful, long-term relationship card that he wasn't seeing anyone. Maybe he's been doing the same as me and not doing it right under my nose. "So what exactly are you saying here?" Lilly asks, pulling me from my thoughts and bringing my focus back to them. "That Taylor has to keep it in his pants to prove to you he can change his slutty ways while you're out there getting your rocks off?"

"I hadn't thought of it like that," Caleb admits quietly.

"It's a bit hypocritical, Caleb. Taylor is who he is, and his past is his past. None of that is anything you can change. But like I said, he's different with you. You might just need to stop making excuses and take a leap of faith."

I watch as Caleb lifts his mug to his mouth slowly, clearly lost in his thoughts. I wish I could read his mind.

"That smells amazing," I announce as I round the corner making my presence known.

Lilly looks up and smiles brightly but Caleb flinches and looks up like he's seen a ghost.

"Hey," I say, smiling at him as I walk in and take a seat at the table next to him.

His lip twitches up in response but he doesn't say anything. His eyes bore into mine though like they are trying to figure something out. It makes me wonder if the conversation that he just had with Lilly might make a difference or if he's just curious as to whether I heard any of it or not.

"Lilly, that was incredible," I announce with a hand on my belly after polishing off not only a full fry up but also her famous homemade pancakes topped with fresh fruit, syrup and cream.

Caleb adds his praise for her cooking before falling quiet once again. He's barely said anything since I walked in the room. I wish I knew where his head's at.

"We should probably head back soon," I say to Caleb a while later. We'd been sat in Lilly and Lucas's conservatory overlooking their very well kept garden as we chatted about life. No more was said about what happened yesterday. Lilly knows better than to keep on about it. This isn't the first time she has dealt with the aftermath of something like this. And Caleb, well he's way too lost in his own head right now I think.

"I need to get back for that shoot tomorrow but I think maybe you should stay for a few days. Chill out, recover, spend some more time with Lilly," he says sadly.

"I've got work," I add, reminding him that life doesn't stop just because I've got a few bruises. Plus *that* shoot he's talking about is an underwear shoot for a pretty well known designer that Caleb and a leggy blonde he often works with have landed. It's a pretty big deal for him. Him telling me all about it excitedly the day he got the call isn't the only reason I know all about it. I may just have managed to convince everyone at work that it would be a great high profile job for me to assist with. So that means I get to spend tomorrow afternoon and probably the day after basically staring at Caleb in just his teeny tiny undies. Is there a better way to spend a day? Probably not!

Not only do I have no intention of missing that opportunity I also don't want to allow him to go home without me. I feel like something changed between us this morning and I can only hope and pray that Caleb's conversation with Lilly this morning's also helped. I'm not risking him going home alone, overthinking it and possibly changing whatever decision it is he might be coming to.

It doesn't ever escape my attention that I call his flat home. I'm more comfortable in his flat than anywhere I've lived before. I thought the flat with Lilly in Cheltenham felt like home but Caleb's is different, better. I guess that's another reason why I've never left or made any attempt to.

---

11 months ago...

Living and working in London has always been a pipe dream. I want the opposite of the small village I grew up in. I want hustle and bustle. I want vibrancy. I want to not be the only gay in the village. Even though knowledge of that fact was kept a hushed secret because my wanker stepdad is not only an abusive arsehole he is also homophobic.

I'd been researching possible photography jobs in London for a long time in the hope something would appear at the right time for me. But it wasn't happening and I was beginning to get disheartened. Maybe it wasn't meant to be.

Then I went to spend the night with Caleb and remembered why I loved London. I remembered everything I'd said I wanted and I knew I couldn't give up getting there. I'd be perfectly happy living in a shithole flat like he was just so I could say I was living my dream. I may have taken the piss out of where he was living but I totally understood what he was doing.

I got chills the second I looked at the photographs he'd left out on the coffee table. It wasn't only because he looked incredible but the style of the photographs just spoke to me. Yes I was excited about looking at Caleb laid out on that decorators table in only his underwear but in that moment I felt a renewed belief that I could do it. That I could find my way to a life where I would be taking photographs like that.

I continued staring at the array of photographs laid out before me but Caleb soon rushed over and scooped them up. I could tell he was embarrassed by them, the thought made me laugh. He never needs to be embarrassed of looking that good. Before he took all of them I managed to get a good look at the back of one he dropped. I needed to know who was taking those photographs and I needed to get in touch with them.

"Can I speak to Mr. Bentley-Cox please?" a very polite woman asks when I put my phone to my ear.

My hazy eyes focus on the alarm clock next to my bed and alert me to the fact it's only just gone 9 AM. Who the hell rings me this early in the morning?

"Yes," I manage before clearing my throat. My mouth feels like the bottom of a bird's cage. I knew those shots last night were a bad idea.

"Mr. Bentley-Cox, it's Carly calling from Capture Photography about your recent application."

Suddenly I'm wide-awake and sat bolt upright in bed.

"Yes."

"Unfortunately your application for junior photographer hasn't been successful—"

All the breath I was holding in hope comes out in one big rush as the disappointment settles in. I knew it was a *long shot. I've got no real experience so this was what I was expecting, really.*

"Okay, well, thank you for letting me know," I say, disappointment obvious in my voice. "Goodbye." I go to hang up but my name being called down the phone stops me.

I put it back to my ear. "Yeah?" I ask.

"Please, let me finish. Your application for that job was unsuccessful but—" I feel all my hope bubble back up to the surface with that one but. "Paul and Nancy were really impressed with you. They would like to offer you an assistant job to get you the experience you need to hopefully progress in the future."

"Are you fucking joking?" I respond, totally unprofessionally.

Thankfully it makes her laugh before she says, "No Mr.—"

"It's Taylor."

"Okay, well, no, Taylor, I'm not joking. They loved you and your work and would love for you to join the team."

"Fuck me!"

"I'm okay," she says, again with a laugh. "Do you need a moment? I can ring back with details when it's settled in," she offers.

"No, I'm fine. It was just a bit of a shock. Go on," I prompt, wanting to know all the details.

"I know it's short notice but Paul and Nancy would like you to start in two weeks. We know you're not in the area so they have said they will help with accommodation

in the short term if you need it. Is that going to be possible?"

"YES!" I shout because I'd make it work if they wanted me there tomorrow. "Can I let you know about the accommodation?"

"Of course. I will put everything in writing and send it out this afternoon. Please have a good read through and if you're happy can you sign and send back please?"

"Yes. I can't believe it," I say, still shocked.

"Well, believe it. And if I didn't say it before, congratulations. I think you'll fit in very well around here."

I thank her before hanging up. I fall back against my pillow still grinning like an idiot. I flip over, shove my face into my pillow and scream. I have no idea if Lilly's here or not but I don't want to wake her if she is. I can't fucking believe this. It's happening, it's really happening.

I have no idea what the pay is and I really don't care. I'll get a second job if needs be. All I know is that I've landed myself a job working alongside some seriously talented photographers.

When I researched the company after getting back from Caleb's I learnt that they're a relatively small company started by a husband and wife team a few years ago. They've since grown and have landed some incredible contracts in the fashion industry. When I saw that they were advertising I couldn't believe my luck. I didn't think I stood a chance alongside all the other experienced photographers that were sure to apply but I went for it anyway. When I got the call to go to an interview I thought they were joking, a little like a few minutes ago. I didn't tell anyone about the interview. If no one knew about it then no one would know when I didn't get it. I was not expecting this.

Once I'm a little calmer I get myself dressed and head to the kitchen to get a coffee. I've got stuff to organise if I'm going to move my life to London in two weeks.

"Taylor, it's been a while," Caleb greets when he answers my call.

"I know, sorry. It's been crazy finishing up uni," and shagging my way around Cheltenham trying to forget about you, *I think but don't say out loud.*

"No worries. Everything go okay?"

"Yes, just waiting for my final grade. Listen, I need a favour," I say, getting straight down to business.

"Go on."

"I've landed myself a job in London. Any chance of crashing on your sofa for a few weeks until I find my own place? They want me to start in two weeks and I'm not going to be able to get anywhere sorted that quickly."

"Uh," Caleb answers sceptically.

"You'd be doing me a massive favour. I promise to be out of your hair as soon as possible," I say, almost begging. I've no idea if this is a good idea or not but I'd much rather stay with Caleb than wherever my new bosses have in mind.

"A couple of weeks?"

"Yes. Just until I sort something out for myself."

"Okay. You won't need to sleep on the couch though. I've moved."

"What? I was looking forward to walking through the piss-scented stairwell everyday. Where are you now?"

"Wow, how much are they paying you for that body?" I ask as Caleb opens his new front door for me. From the second I exited the tube station I could tell I was in a much nicer area than when I first visited him.

"Enough," he answers as he takes one of my bags from me. "Is this all you've got?"

"Yeah, I don't own much shit." When I moved out of my childhood home I took only what I needed and I've never had the money to add to my small collection of stuff.

"This is your room," Caleb says as he drops the bag he's carrying onto the bed.

"Thank you, Caleb. I really appreciate this."

"You're welcome, I think." He still looks and sounds very unsure about letting me stay here.

"What're you worried about?"

He looks down at his bare feet before letting out a breath. "That I'll come home to find you with a different man every night."

"Caleb," I say on a sigh. "I know how I've acted before but this is your flat. I wouldn't." I don't say what I really want to say in fear he changes his mind about me staying but the only person I want to be shagging in this flat is him. I hoped maybe some time apart would've helped change his mind but as he stands in the doorway to the room I'm going to be sleeping in for the next few weeks he looks as closed off as ever.

"I've got a shoot down south all week so you've got the place to yourself."

"Oh, okay." My heart drops at the thought of spending my first few days in London alone.

"Get up to whatever you want to in this room. But nothing anywhere else."

"Caleb," I say as he turns to leave. "That warning isn't necessary. I know what you think of me but I'm going to show you that you're wrong."

"We'll see."

Present...

"Pull over in the next services," I demand.

"Sure," Caleb mutters quietly.

We left Lilly's a few hours ago and the journey has been pretty much silent. My memories of what Caleb thinks of me along with what I heard him say to Lilly earlier have my anger simmering on the surface. I thought he could see through all that now.

"Go on then," he says when he pulls the car to a stop. He looks up at me when I don't go to leave the car. "What? Don't you want a piss or something?"

"No. I want you to tell me what the fuck's going on in your head. This morning you made me think something was changing and now you're all cold and acting like you don't even want to be breathing the same air as me."

"It's nothing. Nothing's changed."

"But it has. You can't tell me there wasn't something this morning. I may have had the shit kicked out of me but I'm not fucking stupid, Caleb. I know what I saw, what I felt."

"Well, I'm sorry I gave you the impression it had. Because nothing's changed you're still—" He stops mid sentence but I finish it for him.

"A whore."

"I knew you were listening to our conversation this morning. How dare you? That was private."

"So private you had it at the dining room table for me to hear. I can't believe that after all this time you still think that of me. What exactly have I done to make you still think that?"

Caleb opens his mouth to answer but no sound comes out.

"Lilly was right. You're a hypocrite. So what I've had sex a handful of times since moving to London and once you caught me in the act. That doesn't make me a FUCKNG WHORE," I shout before swinging the door open and get out of the car for some air. I'm so fucking angry.

When I moved to London I knew a new lifestyle was needed. But I didn't stop my bed-hopping ways because of Caleb and what he thought of me. I stopped it for me. I wanted to focus on my career and if I'm honest spending night after night in other people's beds wasn't making me happy.

I pace back and forth in front of the car for a few minutes. I can feel Caleb's stare on me but I don't meet his eyes. Eventually I come to rest with my arse perched on the bonnet.

I feel the car move beneath me as Caleb gets out but I don't look up.

"I'm sorry, Taylor. I didn't mean it."

"Yes you did. That's all you've ever seen me as. A whore who bed-hops whenever he wants to. I thought you'd seen more to me than that. But clearly I was wrong." I stand up and go to move back toward the passenger side of the car. "I think it's time I found myself somewhere else to live," I say over my shoulder.

Suddenly my wrist is grasped and I'm turned and pushed back against the car. I don't get a chance to do anything before I feel his lips against mine. I want to push him away. I should but I don't because the second I feel his tongue open my lips to allow him entry I sag back against the car and let the feelings that Caleb ignites in my body take over.

Without any instruction from my brain my tongue tangles with his and I tilt my head to deepen the kiss. One of his hands comes up to rest at the back of my head and the other slides under the fabric of my t-shirt and stops on my waist. The feel of his hand against my skin leaves a tingling trail behind it.

He steps toward me pressing my body between his and the car, I suck in a breath as pain shoots out from my ribs but he thankfully doesn't notice. I feel him as hard against me as I am. Fuck I've waited too fucking long to kiss him again.

Someone wolf-whistling in the distance brings us to our senses, making him pull back and step away from me. I look at him but he keeps his eyes down on the floor.

"We should get going," he says before marching back around to the driver's side.

I continue to lean back against the side of his car for a few more seconds to try to recover from his kiss.

It's not until I'm buckled in and ready to go that Caleb finally looks over at me.

"I'm sorry. I shouldn't have done that."

"No you're right, you probably shouldn't," I agree because he's started something now. He's lowered his walls and allowed me to see what he really wants.

Caleb

I kissed him.

I fucking kissed him.

I've held myself back all this time and it's his pathetic bruised face and a threat of moving out that has me caving to what I really want.

The tension in the car was awful before but now, after that kiss, it's unbearable.

Why the fuck did I kiss him?

I don't even know why I'm questioning myself. I know why I kissed him. I've wanted to feel his lips against mine for a long fucking time but I never allowed it. I convinced myself about not wanting him with his whorish ways but I knew it was all a bullshit excuse. It wasn't until Lilly called me out on it earlier that I realised what shit I was telling myself. I knew he'd slept with at least one guy since living with me because I came home from a shoot and caught them at it when I went to his room to ask if he wanted to go for a drink. The image of him deep inside another guy still haunts me. I hated my reaction, the jealousy that bubbled up inside me. So I continued with my *Taylor is a whore and I don't want him* mentality. Lilly was right, though. I'm a total hypocrite because I've been with a couple of guys. Only when I've been away, mind you. If I hadn't then I certainly would have ended up in Taylor's room. I got close a few nights. I'm embarrassed to admit that I've found myself stood in the hallway between our rooms arguing with myself more than once.

I'm totally lost in my own head and before I know it we are pulling up outside our apartment. The only words spoken on the rest of the journey were my apology and Taylor's warning. I'm not sure if it was meant as a warning but the way he said it with his voice even deeper than usual gave me the impression that I'd started something that I'm pretty sure I'm going to be incapable of stopping.

The second the car comes to a stop Taylor is out of the car and gathering the bags from the boot. It doesn't escape my attention that he doesn't move quite as smoothly as he usually would. It's impossible to forget what he went through on Friday with the bruises and cuts on his face but I keep underestimating how much the rest of him must hurt.

I lock the car and jog up the stairs to catch up with him. He doesn't look back but he knows I'm there because I hear him say, "I didn't think you were coming."

I know it's not what he means but my brain takes that simple statement and runs with it, fuck how badly do I want to be coming?

My silence makes him turn around when we get to our front door. The look on my face must tell him exactly what I'm thinking because he leans in and whispers in my ear, "all in good time."

Before I know what's happening the bags have been dropped, the front door has been slammed and I'm backed up against it.

"Don't even think about trying to stop this. You started it, so I'm going to finish it," he warns before his lips descend on mine.

All the fight and bullshit I've been telling myself about why this is a bad idea fall away when I feel his skin on mine.

His fingers start working on the buttons on my shirt as his tongue continues to duel with mine. It's only seconds before I feel his hands on my shoulders pushing my shirt away. The feeling of his hands running down my chest and over my stomach has tingles shooting around my body. When he gets to my waist he grips tight and starts to pull me toward his room.

We are still connected at the lips, neither of us willing to end the kiss that has been building up for years quite yet.

I hear a thud as he kicks open the door before I'm forcefully pushed away from him. The backs of my knees hit his mattress and I fall down onto his bed.

Taylor reaches behind him and pulls his t-shirt over his head gently, revealing his stunning muscular torso to me. The one he's been taunting me with by walking around practically naked since he moved in. I have dreamt about how all those muscles will feel under my hands more than once.

"Are you sure about this?" I ask in a husky voice when I see the purple and yellow bruising covering his tanned skin.

"More than you can ever imagine," he answers as he unties his jogging bottoms and drops them to the floor. He is gorgeously naked underneath; his cock is hard and begging for me.

As much as I want to drop to my knees in front of him I'm frozen to the spot as I take in the sheer perfection in front of me.

Taylor is stacked. I've always known this but seeing him totally naked, he seems even bigger even more intimidating. I get a sudden bolt of nerves. What if I'm not good enough for him? I've had my fair share of experience when I was in America but it's nowhere near the amount Taylor's had. This thing between us has been building for a long time, what if it's not as good as I've been imagining—hoping—for?

Shit.

I feel my shoulders sag a little and I'm just about to back out when Taylor speaks.

"Well? What are you waiting for?" he asks as he grasps his cock in his palm.

"Fuck," I say as I let out a huge breath. I suddenly have a huge desire to go and find his camera.

"Caleb?"

"Sorry," I mutter and I see his eyes widen in panic.

My apology isn't because I'm about to back out though, it's for how long I've kept him waiting—kept myself waiting.

I drop from the bed down onto my knees so I'm eye level with his cock. It's fucking huge, like the rest of him, yet fucking perfect.

I rip my gaze away from it and slowly make my way up his body until I'm staring up into his dark eyes that are looking down on me with a mixture of hunger, lust and danger in them. I don't see his cut eyebrows or the bruising covering his gorgeous face. All I see is him. Taylor. A man who has been driving me fucking crazy since I first saw him across the room that New Year's Eve.

Taylor blinks and breaks our stare. I use the opportunity to take him in my hand. I pump him up and down a couple of times before leaning forward and licking around the tip of his cock.

He lets out a hiss at my contact, his hand threads into my hair and his fingers grip painfully hard. He forces my head forward so I have no choice but to part my lips and take him in my mouth. He's hot and as smooth as silk against my tongue. I suck and lick at him like my life depends on it while he chants my name above me. Bringing him almost to his knees with this one simple act makes me feel more powerful and important than I ever have in my life.

I'm completely lost to what I'm doing when my head gets pulled back away from him. I open my mouth to ask what's wrong but he beats me to it.

"It's not ending that way. Not this time anyway." The insinuation that this isn't a one time only thing has a weird mix of excitement and anxiety bubbling up in my stomach. I've known for a long time now that Taylor could well be the one I've been looking for but I can't help the fear I have that this isn't what he's looking for. Fear that when the time came and I caved to my need for him that it would be the beginning of the end for us. For whatever relationship it is we have here.

I feel his fingers brush the skin just above my waistband and I realise that he's pulled me so I'm standing right in front of him.

"I should warn you, I don't do soft and I certainly don't do gentle," he says in my ear. His words make my breathing falter and goosebumps prick my skin.

I try to swallow but my throat is suddenly very dry. "O... Okay."

He tugs my jeans open before shoving them down my legs along with my boxers. He lowers down so he can pull my shoes off and slide the fabric down and away from my legs. He's just about to stand back to full height when I feel him grasp the back of my thighs and lift me. He lifts me so my legs would go around his waist but I don't get a chance to do just that because he throws me back onto the bed.

As I bounce on the mattress a couple of times his previous words repeat in my head, *"I don't do soft and I certainly don't do gentle."* He certainly wasn't lying.

I prop myself up on my elbows just as he pulls something from his bedside cabinet and begins crawling up the bed between my legs.

"Perfect," I mutter but I don't mean to say it aloud.

"Really?" Taylor asks with a very smug fucking smile

on his face. My cheeks heat instantly with embarrassment. "Too late for that. You're already laid naked on my bed with your cock out," he comments as he settles himself on his knees between my open legs.

He reaches out and takes hold of my cock. I throw my head back as my entire body melts into the bed. "Too long," I whimper, thinking about how long it's been since I saw some action.

"Perfect, you'll be nice and tight for me."

My eyes fly open at his comment. I've only bottomed once before and that was with my first boyfriend when I was a teenager. Since him I've always preferred to be the one in charge.

Taylor's smile only gets bigger when he sees my reaction. "Oh, Caleb. We are going to have so much fun," he says with a small chuckle.

He shifts himself so he's laying on his front. I expect him to take me in his mouth but instead he goes lower and I feel his tongue tease between my ass cheeks.

"Ah fuck," I groan when he goes a bit deeper at the same time as stroking my cock.

I bend my knees and put my feet flat on the bed to give him better access. He continues with his tongue for a few minutes before he swaps to use his fingers, having lubed me up enough.

His finger teases at my entrance before slowly sliding inside a little.

"Relax," he encourages when he feels me tense up. He leans over me and takes my mouth in a kiss that is totally opposite of the rough ride he promised me.

Soon I'm like putty in his hands. I completely submit to him and the feels he's igniting in my body.

He pulls back from the kiss and looks down at me for a few seconds. His eyes are darker than I've ever seen before. He sits up straight and removes his hands from me. I almost feel naked without it. I watch as he picks up the condom he grabbed earlier and rolls it down his cock before squeezing a generous amount of lube on it.

He moves himself into position and in no time I feel him pressing at my entrance.

"Stay relaxed for me," he whispers in my ear after he's folded himself back over me.

His breath on my neck makes me shiver but it only lasts a second or two because I feel him begin to push inside. I suck in a breath and will my body to relax.

Taylor's hand slides under my neck and tips my head back. He kisses the corner of my mouth before sucking on my bottom lip. He bites down as he thrusts a little more.

"That's it," he mutters before lifting my head so my lips connect with his. He holds me to him as he kisses me deeper than he has before.

When he pulls back I realise it was totally a distraction technique because he's slowly sliding in and out of me, and fuck me it feels incredible.

"Fuck, Caleb," he grates out as he sits up straight.

"Uh-huh," is the only noise I can make as I feel every inch he's giving me.

His hands run down my thighs and one of them grabs my cock again, which is lying begging for release against my stomach.

"Uh fuck," I groan as his giant hand strokes me. My

orgasm hits me all of a sudden and I feel like a fucking teenager again coming way too soon. My cock pulsates in Taylor's hand as I cover my stomach.

"Fuck, that was hot," Taylor says as he stares down at my stomach. "My turn," is the only warning I get before he ups his tempo until he's fucking me into the mattress.

It's not long before I'm hard again and feel another orgasm building. I take it upon myself to fist my cock this time. Taylor's too engrossed in chasing his own pleasure. The sight of him thrusting in and out of me with his head thrown back and his muscles pulled tight is too much and a few strokes later I'm coming again.

"You make me feel like a teenager," I admit into his neck a few minutes later. I can only describe the sound as a roar that Taylor made when he came inside me. The image was so fucking feral it sends shivers down my spine just thinking about it. He immediately fell on top of me, a panting sweaty mess. I couldn't think of a fucking better place to be than underneath him right now.

I feel his body shudder with his laughter. "I fucking loved it," he comments as he pulls out of me slowly and rolls over on to his side. "You come as much as you like, as long as it's me you're doing it for." He props himself up on his elbow after disposing of the condom over the side of the bed and looks down at me.

"I knew it would be worth the wait but I really could've done with that a long time ago."

I smile at him sleepily because I don't want to admit that maybe I've been wrong all this time. If I went home with him that night then maybe I would have found what

I'd been looking for back then. The reasons I didn't do that aren't far from my mind though.

"Don't look at me like that, Caleb."

"Like what?" I ask innocently.

"Like you're regretting it already. I'm not going to do anything stupid now I've got you here. You have to trust me."

My heart beats a little faster hearing those words but my mind's still telling me not to trust him. He's a great friend, an amazing person, but I still have this fear that he's going to rip me apart.

"Trust me, Caleb," he begs. "I want this. I want this as much, if not more, than you do."

"Okay," I whisper before stretching up and kissing him gently. I really hope he's right.

Chapter 4

Taylor

I roll over and stretch my arm out to find him. What I find instead though is a cold and empty other half of the bed. I sit myself up on my elbow and look around the room.

He's done a runner!

And to think, I'm the one with the bad reputation.

I try to give him the benefit of the doubt so I swing my legs over the side of the bed and head out to the living area of his flat. That's empty so I move toward his bedroom hoping he's in his en suite shower. That could actually be pretty perfect I think as I glance down at my bobbing morning wood. I'm majorly disappointed when I get there and find it empty and looking unused.

"Caleb, where the fuck are you?" I mutter to myself as I head into the kitchen to make a coffee. I know he often goes to the gym before a shoot but after yesterday I really didn't think he'd just up and leave without so much as a goodbye kiss... or blow job.

Fuck, his mouth on me yesterday was so good.

I fist my cock as I stand waiting for the coffee machine to wake up. I see movement out of the corner of my eye and look up. Staring back at me from her kitchen is our nosey neighbour across the street in just a towel. I'm unsure if she looks fascinated or concerned with my body covered in colourful bruises.

Fuck!

I give her a quick wave before moving away from the window behind me that's allowing her to see me in all my naked glory. I'm confident it's not the first time she's seen my bare arse but I don't need to give her the wrong idea. I may have indulged in one or two, or loads, women in my time but they were just a body when I needed one. Women are gorgeous, all those soft curves, but it's men that really get me going. Hard lines, muscles, cocks. Well if I'm being honest it's not men, it's one man. One man who left my bed while I was sleeping. I really fucking hope he's not regretting it already. He's spent so long fighting what's between us that I guess doing a one-eighty isn't going to go as smoothly as I thought it might.

I glance up at the clock and see that in just over an hour I will see him at the studio for his shoot. At least I should be able to read his reaction to me being there even if I don't get a chance to talk to him.

I finish making myself a coffee before heading for a shower to sort myself out.

Although I think I'm early I'm actually the last to the studio. Everyone's already getting everything set up. The shoot is happening in an old warehouse with massive windows overlooking the city behind. The props are all vintage. There's an array of old looking light fittings, ladders and furniture. Unfortunately Caleb is nowhere to be seen.

"What the fuck happened to you?" Paul says when he looks up at me. Until I saw the look on his face I'd almost forgotten about the state of mine.

"It's nothing. I got jumped on Friday afternoon," I lie smoothly.

"Shit. Did you get a look at them, call the police?"

"No, they were gone as quick as they came. I wouldn't be able to identify them."

"That's shit. Are you sure you're okay to be here? That looks pretty sore," he asks, nodding toward my face.

"I'm fine. I'd rather be distracted than sat focusing on it."

"Fair enough. Right, go get the equipment, the van's just outside," he instructs and I head off to do as I'm told, pleased that my first job of the day isn't to find the nearest coffee shop.

Unfortunately that request comes in once I have the contents of the van inside the studio. I grab my notebook and take everyone's coffee and breakfast orders before leaving feeling disappointed. I strung out asking for everyone's orders for as long as I could but Caleb didn't appear and I couldn't put off going any longer.

When I get back laden down with coffee and Danish pastries the photo shoot is in full swing. I take a few seconds to appreciate the body under the spotlight at the other side of the room. The lighting is perfect and picks up every line and muscle of his lean body. The only problem is that he isn't alone. Leah is stood way too close for my liking with her hands on his chest. It takes a while for me to identify the feeling that starts weighing me down the longer I stand there looking at them but I soon realise it's jealousy. I've never been jealous over a man before and I'm not sure I like it. Sure there've been times in my life where I've been jealous of others. I used to look at other kids at school and wish my life was like theirs. To be fair I would have had any life that didn't include my stepdad. But this kind of jealousy is new.

Someone barks an order making Caleb and Leah move and for me to step farther into the room. My movement catches Caleb's attention and his eyes narrow slightly as they lock on to mine. I've no idea if he's pissed off or just shocked to see me. I'm hoping for the latter and that it's a nice surprise but I'm not so sure.

"Are you waiting for them to get cold before you give them to us?" some smart-arse asks when they see me with my arms full of their coffee.

I swear to God, when I do get promoted I will never talk to any assistant the way some of these lot do to me on a shoot. The majority of the photographers I work with are incredible. It's the others, the creative directors and the models. It's like I'm a piece of shit on their shoe.

I politely dish out the coffees hoping I give the correct one to each person before joining Paul where he is changing the lens on his camera.

I look at the set up of the shoot and around the room for a few minutes before I notice something. "Wouldn't it be better to shoot over in that corner, I know the window wouldn't be in the background but the light is incredible."

Paul looks over to where I'm pointing and pauses for a minute before agreeing with me. "Good shout, Taylor.

Let's let this guy do his thing," he says referring to the man clearly in charge of this shoot, "before suggesting changes but I think you're right."

I thought spending the day watching Caleb do his thing would be awesome unfortunately by the time the day is out, I'm aching, fed up and exhausted. Oh and a little frustrated that I've spent hours looking at that body but not been able to touch.

"Hey, any chance of a ride home?" I ask after knocking on Caleb's dressing room door. He's stood in front of a mirror rough drying his hair with a towel and wearing only a pair of boxers. The sight improves my mood instantly.

"You didn't want to mention that you'd swindled a job here today then?" he asks, sounding a little pissed off and completely ignoring my question.

"I arranged it weeks ago. I thought it would be fun."

"Fun?"

"Yeah, spending the day staring at you seemed like a good idea." I see him soften a little with my answer.

"Seemed like a good idea?"

"Yeah well I kinda forgot I'd end up spending the day being bossed around and having to look at you from a distance when I know how fucking good this body feels under my hands," I explain as I step up to him and run my hand around his hip to grab on to his arse.

"Taylor," he warns.

"What? No one can see us."

"It's not that."

"Oh no you don't. You're not backing away after last night."

"I just—"

"Don't trust me. I know. Let me prove myself to you. Please," I say. "I'm willing to get on my knees and beg if necessary," I add with a wink.

Caleb doesn't respond so I go to drop to the floor, more than willing to prove this point to him. I didn't get a chance to taste him last night and that is something I want to rectify as soon as possible.

Before I get very far Caleb reaches out and grabs my forearm. "Not here. Let's go get dinner." I almost argue but I'm fucking starving, and not just for him so I agree and wait while he gets dressed.

"Taylor?"

"Yeah?" I ask lifting my head from where it was resting against the wall.

"Maybe we should order a takeaway!" Caleb says with a smile.

I fell asleep on the sofa not long after I'd polished off the curry Caleb ordered when we got home last night. I vaguely remember him pulling me from the sofa and depositing me in my bed. I was disappointed when I realised he didn't stay with me but I was so exhausted that I soon fell straight back to sleep.

Thankfully I wake to the sound of him banging around in the kitchen.

"Hey, sleep well?" he asks when I appear in the doorway a few minutes later.

"Like you wouldn't believe."

"I think I would from the snoring coming from your room," he says with a laugh.

"Come here," I say as I reach out and grab the fabric of his t-shirt in my fist and pull him to me.

"Morning breath," he says, turning his head away from me. "Brush your teeth and then I'll consider it."

"You'll consider it?" I ask with a raised eyebrow. "You don't get a choice," I say over my shoulder as I make my way to the bathroom to do as I'm told.

"Better?" I ask when I reappear. I blow a stream of minty fresh breath into his face and wait for confirmation.

"Ugh, if I have to," he tries to say seriously but his twitching lip gives him away.

I repeat my earlier move and pull him to me with his t-shirt. "I like this," I admit when he's flush against me.

"What's that exactly?"

"This. You. Being able to do this," I say before lowering my lips to his.

"How long until we have to leave?" I ask when I eventually pull back from our kiss.

"Twenty minutes."

"Plenty of time," I say as I begin to push him in the direction of my bedroom.

"No it's not and I need a shower."

"You smell perfect to me, at least let me get you all sweaty before you shower."

"Taylor, no, we haven't got time," he says seriously while trying to shove me away from him.

"You're serious?"

"Yes. Delayed gratification is a good thing, it'll be worth it."

"I'm not a patient man, Caleb," I warn as he rushes out of my room.

"That doesn't surprise me," I hear shouted back.

"Fuck's sake," I mutter as I look down at my tented boxers. This is going to be a long arse fucking day.

And I'm right. We're still at the studio well past 8 PM. The shots we get are golden, well Paul and I think so anyway. The director, not so much. He insists we keep reshooting even though we lost the best of the light hours ago.

By the time he calls it a day I'm almost as irritated as I was when we finished yesterday.

"Thank fuck for that," Paul groans next to me as he starts disconnecting all our equipment. "I promised Nancy I'd take her out to dinner tonight. I'm gonna be in the doghouse."

"When aren't you?" I ask with a laugh. We both know that Nancy is way too laid-back and understanding to do such a thing. Especially where work is concerned.

Once we're packed away I go in search of Caleb. I once again find him in his dressing room, only today he hasn't just got out of the shower. He's still in it.

I quietly close the door behind me and turn the lock. I pull my t-shirt over my head and drop it to the floor as I make my way over to the steamed up shower door. I lose my shoes, trousers and boxers just before reaching for the handle. Caleb is stood with his back to me and his face up toward the stream of water. I take a couple of seconds to appreciate that fine arse with water running all over it but

I can only stand there so long because the temptation to touch is too much. I step forward and run my hands down his sides and around to rest on his stomach. He physically jumps and, much to my amusement, screams like a girl.

"It's just me, calm down," I say before kissing across his now slightly stubbly jawline. My hands run down his back and grab on to his arse as I pull him to me. His body lines up perfectly to mine. "Fucking love these lips," I mutter quietly before placing mine against them. I push him back slightly so we're both under the torrent of water.

"Taylor, we can't do this, we're at work," Caleb argues when I eventually let him pull back.

"We've finished. Everything's packed and people are leaving," I say reassuringly as I start to kiss down his neck. "I've been waiting to have you all day." I know he's only arguing because he thinks it's the right thing to do. I can feel his hard cock resting against mine telling me what he really wants. He wants this, he just thinks it's wrong. And that's okay with me because if he's worried about being caught then it'll only make it hotter.

He soon stops trying to disagree when I drop to my knees and immediately take him in my mouth. I watch as the water pours down over his chest and stomach as I work him slowly in and out.

"Taylor," he groans in pleasure and the sound alone has me closer to the orgasm I've been craving all day.

Just before he's about to empty himself in my mouth I pull back and stand up.

"Wha—"

"Turn around, bend over and put your hands on the tiles," I demand.

He immediately does as I ask and I quickly reach for the condom and sachet of lube I dropped on the floor outside the shower door.

In seconds I'm wrapped up and ready to go. I squeeze a blob of lube on my fingers and set about prepping Caleb for a short hard fuck.

He flinches and tenses up when I first touch him but he soon relaxes.

"Ready?" I ask, but I don't give him time to answer because I know he is. Bending my knees I line myself up. I thrust forward and whatever it was that Caleb was about to say comes out as a grunt instead.

His arse is so fucking perfect. If I knew it would be so good I wouldn't have let him keep putting this off as long as he did.

"Fuck, fucking love this," I grunt out between thrusts. "I'm gonna come in your fucking arse, I want to feel you coming too. You ready?"

"Uh... huh... yeah," he agrees.

I reach around and take his cock. I move my hand at the same speed I thrust into him. I feel the first twitch of his approaching orgasm just as my balls draw up and I lose myself entirely. I think I call out but I couldn't fucking tell you if I said anything understandable, or how loud I was.

"Fuck," Caleb pants as he stands and rests his head on his forearm that's leant against the tiled wall.

"Fucking right."

"Leah," Caleb greets as we both step out of his dressing room a while later. She takes one look at us and starts to smile and nod. "What?" he asks but I don't need to hear her answer. The way she's looking at us says it all.

"The walls between the male and female dressing rooms aren't that thick you know," she says with a laugh.

"Shit."

"Don't, it was hot. Until next time," she says before flouncing off into the distance.

"I told you it was a bad idea," Caleb complains.

"Oh shut up. She loved it. I bet she'll get herself off thinking about it later, that's if she hasn't already."

"Ew, really?" Caleb asks as he slaps my shoulder and starts walking out.

"What? It was hot!"

"Fuck's sake, Taylor." I know he's not being serious so I keep quiet and catch up with him. "I owe you dinner, what do you fancy?"

"You."

"I'm being serious."

"Steak.

"I fucking hate this," Caleb announces once we've ordered.

"You hate being out on a date with me?" I ask a little confused about what he's trying to say.

"Are we on a date?" The smile he gives me tells me that it's not being with me out in public that's his problem right now.

"I haven't ever been on one before. Going out for a meal, all this wining and dining stuff hasn't ever really been on my radar before." When I look up and see the grimace on Caleb's face I realise that I need to stop referring to my past if I'm ever going to convince him that isn't who I am now. "Yes, Caleb. I'm pretty sure this is a date. I actually kinda like that you're my first," I say changing tact.

"It's not like I'm going to be involved in many other of your firsts is it?" he says sadly.

"Oh, I don't know. There's a lot of stuff I haven't experienced yet," I say thinking about my lack of any kind of romantic relationship.

"Like what?"

"Holding someone's hand in the street. Being someone's boyfriend. Falling in love." I don't miss the giant swallow Caleb does at my last point. I'm not saying that I'm in love or anything, I'm just merely pointing out that I never have been. I am, however, alluding to the point that I'm pretty sure I could be falling—and falling fast now he's giving me this chance. "So what was it you were going to say?" I ask when it becomes clear he isn't going to respond to my earlier statement.

He blinks a few times and looks around the room as he tries to gather his thoughts. "I hate that everyone's looking at you like you're some kind of thug just because you've got some bruises."

"I hadn't noticed," I admit as I stare directly at him.

"My focus has solely been on you." His mouth drops open a little but I see the corner of his lip twitch.

"Is that so?"

"My focus is always on you. You're always the best looking man in any room and the only one who's bed I want to end up in."

Caleb

The past week's been pretty incredible. Taylor's been everything I hoped and imagined he'd be. I've seen no sign of him wanting anyone else but me and I couldn't be happier. Sex with him is like nothing I've ever experienced before. It's intense. It's not always rough like he warned me about though, there are moments where he's the most gentle and loving guy. The kind of guy I told myself I wanted but convinced myself that Taylor would never be. He holds my hand while we're watching TV at night. He stops and gives me little kisses just because he feels like it. Everything he does strengthens my thoughts about him being the one. If only I could fully trust him. I still have this nagging feeling that he doesn't really want this, that he's going to get bored of me and want to go and find someone else.

"You've got two minutes to get your naked arse into the bedroom," Taylor growls in my ear. "The washing up can wait."

Thankfully I've only had a couple of jobs this week

and they've both been in London. It's meant we've been able to spend as much time together as possible as we both try to adjust to the new us. Taylor seems to have easily fallen into our new routine that involves him sleeping in my room every night instead of his own. I seem to be finding myself questioning everything a little too much. It's like I'm trying to find any excuse possible to prove he doesn't want this. I fucking hate it and I wish I could just enjoy what I've got instead of looking for clues for what's possibly going to happen tomorrow, next week or next month.

I turn and dry my hands on the tea towel as I watch Taylor pull his t-shirt off as he disappears into my bedroom. I follow suit and I'm only in my boxers when I go to step into the room. Unfortunately a knock on the front door halts my progress.

I pull the door open and find two people I was not expecting looking back at me.

"Mum, Dad. What're you doing here?"

"We came down to help Beth out with some last minute wedding plans and thought we'd stop in on the way home. Are you going to invite us in?" Mum asks, taking a small step toward me. I don't get to respond though because another voice sounds out through the flat.

"I said you have two minutes to get your sexy arse in here, what's the hold up, oh!"

Mum's eyes go over my shoulder before she gasps *oh my God* and covers her mouth with her hand. Dad looks over my shoulder for a second before he raises his eyes to the ceiling.

"Fuck, I'll go get dressed," Taylor announces, and I

turn around just in time to see his naked arse disappear back in to the bedroom.

Fuck, fuck, fuck. This was so not how I wanted to have this conversation with my parents.

"I think you should probably do the same, don't you, Son," Dad suggests as he brings his eyes back down to me.

I walk over to where I discarded my clothes not so long ago and pull them on as Mum and Dad walk sheepishly into the apartment.

"Tea, coffee?"

"Yes please," Dad says as Mum is still stood looking shell-shocked.

"Are you still coming to Paris this weekend?" Mum asks, speaking for the first time but my answer gets interrupted by Taylor's arrival.

"I'm so sorry about that."

"I made you a coffee."

"I was actually going to head out. Give you guys some peace."

"No, that's not—"

"I think that's for the best," Dad interrupts.

Before I have a chance to argue Taylor is out of the door leaving me alone with them. I'm not ashamed or embarrassed in any way about my life. There is just something ingrained in me that doesn't want to disappoint my parents. I'm well aware I need to man up and tell them who I really am though.

"So..." Mum prompts, "Are you still coming to your sister's wedding?" It pisses me off somewhat that her main concern here is whether or not I'm going to cause drama at the wedding she's been waiting for.

"Of course I'm still coming. It's my sister's wedding. I wouldn't miss it for the world."

"And what about *him*?"

"What about him?"

"Is he coming?"

"I... uh..." I don't have an answer to that question. I'm well aware that I've put off mentioning to Taylor that I'm going to Paris this weekend. I know he's going to want to come with me and that would mean having this conversation. It seems the part about this conversation has been taken out of my hands now though.

"Caleb, there's no need to look so worried. We've known about... this for a long time," Dad says reassuringly. I look over and give him a small smile because although he seems fine Mum looks anything but happy. "I was worried for a while that you weren't interested in anyone so it's nice to know you're not alone down here."

"This is all new. Taylor and I have only just got together," I admit.

"But he's been your roommate for a long time now."

"Yeah he has. Nothing's happened before now though."

"You should bring him to the wedding."

"I don't think that's such a good idea," Mum interjects.

"Why not?"

"What would your grandparents think?"

"Penny! I'm sorry, Caleb," Dad says apologising on my mum's behalf.

"What? It's true. They won't understand all this,"

Mum says, waving her arm around. "They expect Caleb to get married and have kids, not this."

"Is that what you think they want for me or what you want for me?" I ask, starting to get pissed off.

"I... uh..."

"I can still do those things, Mum. I can get married. I can have kids. Okay so maybe it's not the traditional way you're imagining but so what. I won't live a life just because people expect me to, I want to live the way I want to. I want to do what makes me happy, not you or my grandparents."

Mum totally ignores my rant. At least I presume she ignores it as she decides not to respond. Instead she reaches over to the bags she set down next to the sofa. "Beth wanted us to give you these. She said you were picking up your suit but your tie is in there along with some stuff she can't fit in her and Daniel's cases."

"Right okay," I say, taking the bags from her and looking inside.

"Come on then, Simon. We should be heading home."

"I thought we were going to suggest having dinner."

It's clear from the look on Mum's face that not only has Dad just seriously put his foot in it but she has no intention of hanging around.

I give Mum a kiss on the cheek after saying goodbye. She turns on her heel and starts marching toward the stairway.

"She'll be fine. Just give her some time to get used to the idea. I think although we knew she held out hope that Beth's wedding might not be the only one."

"I can still—"

"I know," he agrees. "Like I said, just give her time."

"Okay, thanks Dad."

"We'll see you soon."

I shut the door behind them and lean back against it. It's weird, I always presumed it would be my dad that would have an issue with me being gay. I know Mum has all these visions of brides and babies but I thought she'd be able to see that all of those things are still in my future, maybe.

I grab my phone and after falling back onto the sofa. I find Taylor's number and hit call. It rings and rings and eventually goes to voicemail.

"Where the fuck are you?" I ask the empty room.

I start thinking about having Taylor there with me for Beth's wedding. It's not something I've allowed myself to think about before because I didn't think it was something I wanted but now my parents know about us I can't help but think I want him by my side.

I try phoning him again but it goes straight to voicemail this time. What the fuck?

An hour later and I'm sat staring at the television although I have no idea what I'm actually watching when the buzzer goes off. I don't even think about it, I just press down the entry button thinking Taylor went out in such a rush that he forgot his keys.

"Hello?" I hear shouted into the flat after I walk off into the kitchen to open a bottle of wine. The voice isn't one I was expecting.

"Hello," I say back, heading to the door.

"I'm looking for Taylor."

"And you are?"

"Matt. Taylor and I usually meet up when I'm in town. I tried ringing him but there was no answer so..."

Knowing that one of Taylor's regular hook-ups is stood not only in front of me but at my front door makes my temper flare.

"He's not here, and he's not interested," I seethe.

"And who are you, his boyfriend? Taylor doesn't do boyfriends. He wasn't wrong about his roommate being hot though, so if you're feeling a little lonely I'm sure I could help," he says as he steps toward me. I presume it's meant to be sexy but there's something about this guy that I really don't like. It may well just be because he's had a taste of what's now mine.

Before I realise it's happening I'm reaching my arm out and swinging the door shut. It slams in his face and I can't help but feel pleased with myself when I hear him complain about his nose. "Your loss. If you change your mind then Taylor's got my number. And if you both want to play then I'm more than game."

I walk away from the door, grab the bottle of wine I'd recently opened and pour myself a huge glass.

Chapter 5

Taylor

Caleb's panic and his mother's disgust was written over their faces when I appeared stark bollock naked earlier. Probably not my finest moment but how the fuck was I suppose to know that Caleb's parents were at the front door?

Hanging around to see what was going to play out wasn't an option. I get enough shit from my own parents, I don't need to get involved with anyone else's, that's for sure.

Everything had been going so smoothly with mine and Caleb's transition into a relationship. I guess it was obvious that something was going to derail us sooner or later. I just didn't expect it to be his parents or the fact he's going away for the weekend and didn't think to tell me.

Seeing his name lighting up my phone again pisses me off. I shut the power off and neck my drink. I thought he was serious about us, that he actually wanted to make a go of this with me. But him not telling me about Paris makes me wonder if I've got it all wrong.

By the time I walk back through our front door it's well past midnight and I'm way past being drunk. I stumble my way down to my bedroom and fall onto my bed.

When I wake up the next morning for work my head is pounding and the room is still spinning. After discovering an empty flat I down a couple of mugs full of strong black coffee and head off in the direction of today's shoot.

It doesn't take long for everyone around me to realise I'm in a stinking mood. Thankfully they keep the coffee orders to a minimum and keep well out of my way.

When I get home the only thing I find is a note on the kitchen worktop.

Matt wants to know when you're available to hook-up.

"FUCK!" I shout into the empty room. I launch my phone and watch as it smashes against the wall before hitting the floor a broken mess. I'd had a few calls from an unknown number but I hadn't thought anything of it. If I'd have known it was Matt I would have answered and told him I wasn't interested. Instead he's turned up here looking for a quick shag. I know Caleb's spent almost every second of the past few days overanalysing everything to confirm his suspicion that I don't want a relationship with him but that isn't the case. To begin with that was all I wanted but things have changed a lot in the last couple of years. Living with him as well as watching Lilly and Lucas's relationship develop has left me thinking that maybe having a boyfriend might not be so bad. Yet he's trying everything to prove that isn't true.

When I retrieve my phone I'm amazed to see that although the screen is smashed to fuck the thing actually works. I unlock it before finding Caleb's number and putting it to my ear.

He doesn't answer and I have no idea if that's because he's doing a shoot, he's ignoring me or he's already fucked off to Paris.

I'm sat eating a tasteless microwave meal when I hear a key pushed into the lock. Seconds later I'm looking at a soaking wet Caleb. His hair is sodden and stuck to his forehead and his white t-shirt is soaked through, clinging to every inch of his body. He stands stock-still in the doorway looking at me. His blue eyes dark and narrow, the longer he stares the more pissed off he looks.

"Thought you would have been making the most of having the flat to yourself," he snarls. "Or has Matt already left."

"Fuck off, Caleb. You don't get to be pissed at me. When the fuck were you going to tell me about Paris?"

"It's none of your fucking business."

"It's none of my fucking business that my boyfriend is fucking off to Paris without even telling me." I watch as Caleb's chin drops open at my use of the word boyfriend.

"Yes, boyfriend, Caleb. Correct me if I'm wrong but that is kind of what I thought was going on here."

"I stupidly thought the same until your booty call appeared at my front door."

"I didn't fucking call him. He's in the army and if and when he's local he gets in contact. If I'd have known the number calling me was him I would have told him I wasn't available."

"Whatever."

"Don't fucking whatever me. Why didn't you tell me about Paris?" I stand up and move so I'm directly in front of him and looking down into his eyes. He's not getting away with bullshitting his way out of this.

"Because I don't have to."

"Fuck you," I say quietly as I lift my hands and push against his shoulders. "You were the one who's been going on about honesty, you're the one with the trust issues yet now I find out you're the one who's been doing the lying."

"Not telling you isn't lying, Taylor," he snaps.

"So when were you going to tell me you were going then?"

Caleb's lips stay sealed which fuels my anger.

"You're going to need to fucking explain this to me because I'm not fucking understanding."

"It's for Beth's wedding," he admits, like it should explain everything.

"And?"

"And..." he pauses. "And you'd have wanted to come."

"Damn fucking right I would've done."

"You saw my mum earlier. Her face when they found us practically naked."

"Oh so this is about being ashamed of me."

"What? No!"

"Then what the fuck is it about?"

"It's about me. It's about me not disappointing them, about not ruining my sister's big day. It's about me not wanting to introduce you to them for you to change your mind and leave me. It's about me, not you, Taylor."

I'm stunned by his words, by his vulnerability. I look into his eyes, trying to show him how serious I am about this, that I have no intention of upping and leaving him.

"I can't bear to go through what my sister went through when she was betrayed by the man she loved, who she thought loved her. If you leave me that is exactly what you are going to do to me, Taylor," he admits so quietly I have a hard time hearing it.

I don't put into words my thoughts about what he was trying to say there with the word love, instead I take the final step toward him and slam my lips down on his. I move with such force that his back hits the door behind him with a thud. My hands come up to cage his head in before descending his body and grabbing on to his arse to pull him even tighter to me.

I kiss him like it's the last chance I'm going to get. It's wet, it's tongues, lips, teeth. It's fucking everything a kiss should be. After a good few minutes I reach down and grab the back of his thighs. I lift him so he has no choice but to wrap his legs around my waist. I thrust my hips forward so he has to feel me against him, the action makes him moan into my mouth. He copies the movement and the friction against my cock has me gagging for him. I pull him from the door and march toward his bedroom. The second his feet touch the floor I grab onto the wet fabric of his t-shirt and start peeling it from his skin. My lips go to his neck before descending down his chest. I continue down and run my tongue along every line and indent I come across.

"Taylor, fuck," Caleb mutters above me.

I rip open his fly and shove the heavy fabric of his jeans down his thighs along with his boxers. His cock springs free right in my face. I lean forward and take him to the back of my throat in one go.

"Shit, shit, fuck," he chants as I start to suck.

I fucking love this, the feel of him, the taste of him. It's fucking everything.

I put everything I have into it and when I sense that he's getting close I bring my hand up and begin playing with his balls.

"Fuck, I'm gonna come," he warns seconds before I feel his cock twitch and his cum hit the back of my throat. When he's finished I pull off with a pop and sit back on my heels.

I look up at Caleb who is stood with his head tipped back, his chest heaving with his heavy breathing, his cock's still bobbing and his jeans are still around his ankles.

"Don't move a fucking inch," I demand before running out of the room.

I'm back in seconds with my most precious belonging in my hands.

"Do you trust me?"

He hesitates.

"Caleb, do you trust me? Yes or no."

"Yes," he whispers.

"I need you to mean it."

"Yes, I trust you," he says more sincerely this time so I take it as my cue.

Click.

"What the fuck was that?" he asks opening his eyes to find me down on my knees with my camera to my face.

"You look so fucking hot."

"If anyone see's them I'll fucking kill you," he threatens.

"You're mine, Caleb. I have no intention of anyone seeing you naked ever again. These are for my personal collection."

"Okay."

I take a few more shots before demanding that he gets on the bed and finishing what I started.

They say make up sex is the best you can have. Ain't that the fucking truth.

"Taylor," I hear, bringing me from my sleep.

"Uh-huh."

"I fly out tomorrow afternoon but there're seats left on a flight Friday morning if you can get off work."

My sleep-fuzzed brain has no fucking clue as to what he's talking about. "What?"

"Paris, Taylor. I want you to come with me."

"What fucking time is it? I ask when I open my eyes and see that it's still dark out.

"Uh… half two. So shall I book you on it?"

"Give me a minute." I put my hand up to pause him because I need to let my brain catch up a little before I answer anything.

"Why aren't you asleep?"

"I was but I woke up and realised that you were right and you should be coming with me."

"Say that again."

"I said I woke up and realised you were—" he stops mid sentence when he sees the smile on my face. "Oh fuck off!"

"I can't, I've got a shoot on Friday. I think you were right before though. If your mum is going to have an issue with us then maybe it's not best to flaunt it in front of her face at your sister's wedding. Maybe a more private meeting would be better."

"I guess. I want you there though."

"I want to, but I don't think it's for the best."

"Yeah, I guess," he agrees sadly.

"I'm sorry," I say as I lean over to kiss him.

"What for?"

"I'm sorry that Matt just turned up. I'm sorry I have a past that you don't like."

"It's okay. These things are going to happen occasionally. I just need to trust that it's in the past."

"It is, Caleb. I want you and only you." And to prove my point I set about showing him just how much I do want him.

I hate saying goodbye to him before I leave for work the next morning knowing I'm not going to see him for days. It's the right decision though. We'll organise something with his parents once the wedding is over.

It's the longest day ever and I'm exhausted by the time I get home late. I can't be arsed with dinner so I grab a packet of Super Noodles from the cupboard and tip them into a bowl along with some boiling water. I leave them to do their thing while I get changed into something more comfortable for a night in front of the TV. My camera sitting on the bedside table catches my eye. The memory of using it last night with Caleb pops into my head so I grab it along with my laptop and head back to the living room.

I'm waiting for the photos to download when the buzzer goes off.

"Hello?"

"Taylor," A weak and pathetic female voice says quietly.

"Mum? Come in." I quickly hit the button to release the main door to the building and I pull our front door open as I prepare for what I'm about to be faced with.

My stomach jumps into my throat when she rounds the top of the stairs.

"Fucking hell, Mum," I say as I reach forward to grab the bag she is dragging along behind her.

"It's fine," she says, waving off her bruised and swollen face as if it's nothing.

"It's not fucking fine." I place my hands gently on her

cheeks and take a closer look at the damage. "Motherfucker. Please tell me you're here because you've left that wanker at last."

"Yes. I left two days ago. I didn't come here right away in case it was the first place he looked. Has he been here?" she asks, looking around the room like he's going to jump out at any moment.

"No, I've not heard anything from him, thank fuck."

"Good, I think I managed to convince him that we weren't talking. I left some things around to make it look like I was heading to Scotland."

"Scotland?" She just shrugs as she gently sits herself down on the sofa. "Broken ribs?" I ask, knowing from experience how much they fucking hurt.

"I think so. Any chance of a glass of wine?" she asks when she clocks my glass of red on the coffee table.

"Sure." I head to the kitchen to get it for her, forgetting all about what I left open for her to see.

"I thought you did fashion photography, not porn."

"Fuck," I groan rushing in to shut my laptop down.

"He's not bad to look at. Someone that I should know about?" she asks with a raised eyebrow. Mum and I have never really had the kind of relationship where we can talk about stuff like this, it feels a little weird to start now.

"Yeah, that's Caleb. My boyfriend," I add proudly.

"Really?"

"Why do you sound so surprised?"

"I'm not surprised, just relieved I guess that everything I've put you through over the years hasn't put you off."

"It's done enough damage, don't you worry. It's taken us a long time to get here thanks to my issues."

"I'm sorry, Tay."

"Don't. Just promise me that things are going to change. Do you have any idea what it's like knowing you're still with him, having God knows what done to you." She drops her head and looks totally defeated. "New start, yeah?"

"Yeah," she agrees but not with the enthusiasm I would hope to hear. "So do I get to meet him?"

"He's not here. He's gone to Paris for the weekend for his sister's wedding."

"Why aren't you with him?"

"It's complicated."

We chat for almost an hour about this and that. It's great to be able to have an open conversation without worrying that he's going to be listening somewhere and take offence to what we're saying.

"Please don't take this as me not wanting you here, but I think it's probably best if you stay in a hotel." Mum looks at me and her eyes begin to fill with water. I feel like an arsehole sending her away but he knows where I live. It wouldn't take much for him to find her here. "It's safer, Mum. I'll pay for it, but I want you somewhere he's not going to find you."

"Okay," she agrees, although I can see she's not happy about it.

Once we've finished our drinks I call a taxi to take us both to a hotel to check her in.

"Could you just pull over here, mate," I say to the taxi

driver when he approaches a supermarket. "I'll be ten minutes."

I jump out the car and jog inside. I quickly find the electronics section and pick a pay as you go phone for Mum to use.

I'm back in the car in a little over five minutes. "Here," I say, handing her the box. "I need you to promise me something though."

"Go on."

"If you change your mind and go back to him, this is the last time I'm ever going to help you."

"Okay," she says weakly.

"I mean it, Mum. I can't keep playing this game. I will help you build a new life, do anything you need me to. But if I have any suspicion that you're even talking to him that will be the end of it."

"Okay."

We get her checked in to a hotel and after making sure she has everything she needs I leave her to it. I decide to walk back home as it's not that far. I'm happy that she seems to have left him. It's more than she's done before but I can't get rid of the nagging feeling that this is only temporary. He's like a rotten fucking smell that never goes away and for some reason Mum seems unable to resist the motherfucker.

I shut the front door behind me and make sure I double-lock it as well as put the bolt across. If she's been gone two days like she said then I'm surprised that he hasn't already been here. Maybe she did a better job of making it look like she's gone elsewhere than I'm giving her credit for.

I barely sleep. Every noise outside every bang from our neighbours has been on alert. I could really do without meeting the wrong side of my stepdad's fists again so soon.

I must drift off eventually because when I wake the next morning it's to my ringing phone. I only managed a few texts to Caleb yesterday. He rang once he got to his hotel but I was too busy dealing with Mum to answer. Then when I rang him it went straight to voicemail so I sent him a text to give him a run down of what was happening here.

"Morning."

"What the hell, Tay? Your mum's there?"

"Well in a hotel, yeah. She looks like shit."

"What about him?"

"Fuck knows. She said she made it look like she was heading up north but I can't shake the feeling that he's too clever to fall for something like that."

"I have a huge favour to ask that might just help getting you out of harm's way."

"Oh yeah?" I ask sceptically.

Caleb

"Beth, what's wrong?" Mum shouts in a panic the second we walk into my sister's hotel room and find her sobbing on the bed. The wedding is being held in this swanky hotel that one of Daniel's friends owns. I've stayed in my fair share of hotels but never one this flash. I couldn't believe it when I walked in my room yesterday evening to see the Eiffel Tower looking back at me from the window.

"The photographer's mum has died and he's cancelled. This is a disaster," she splutters.

"Oh honey, it's okay. We can find another, I'm sure."

"Not like him. He was the best."

I don't hear Mum's response; a plan is too busy forming in my head.

"I'll sort it," I announce much to their surprise.

"How are you going to sort it?" my sister snaps. "Know many French photographers, do you?"

"Just trust me," I say before pulling my phone out of my pocket and walking out to the hallway.

Hearing Taylor tell me about his mum makes me realise this is the perfect plan to get him out of the way in case his dickhead stepdad appears again and it solves Beth's photographer problem.

"We need you. Beth's photographer has had to cancel and she's having a meltdown about it. I just booked you a ticket on that flight I mentioned. It should get you here just in time."

"Are you having a laugh?"

"No. Go drag your suit out and get your ass on that plane."

"I've got work, Caleb, and Mum to deal with."

"Call in sick. And she's an adult who can look after herself. Come on, I need you and my mum will love you for saving the day," I add on.

"For fuck's sake, Caleb. I'm on my way. Send me the flight details. It's a good job I lo—"

The air thickens and the buzzing on the line is suddenly the only noise I can hear. My heart thuds in my chest and I repeat the beginning of that sentence over and over in my head. Did he just... Was he going to say...

After long seconds of silence I eventually manage to breathe some air into my lungs and agree to send him what he needs before hanging up. A huge smile breaks out across my face as I hang up the phone. Is Taylor falling in love with me? I push aside the thought that he could have just meant it in a friend kind of way. Surely he wouldn't have cut himself off so abruptly if that was the case though, would he?

"Why are you so happy?" Mum asks when I reappear.

"Photographer's on his way."

"Seriously?" Beth asks, sounding shocked. Does she have that little faith in me?

"Yes, seriously."

"And he's good?"

"Yes, Beth. Now chill out and try to enjoy your day."

Just over four hours later and I'm stood in the hotel foyer waiting for Taylor to emerge from a cab. I was going to meet him at the airport but I stupidly mentioned the idea in front of Beth and she almost had a heart attack in case I got stuck in traffic or something and missed the wedding. I agreed because I'm a soft touch where my sister's concerned and also I thought Taylor's arrival should probably be a surprise for Mum and if I disappeared she might start questioning what was going on. So I resorted to sitting on one of the plush velvet couches with my knee bouncing in excitement and anticipation of what Mum's going to think about this, about having Taylor attend her big day.

I'm on my feet the second I see him step out of the cab. "You're here," I state as I rush toward him.

"Did I have a choice?" he replies with a laugh.

"Come on, Beth's getting ready and wants photos taken from about two hours ago."

"Do I at least get a kiss first?" Taylor asks as he grabs my hand and tugs until I'm chest to chest with him.

"I'm sure that can be arranged," I whisper before reaching up to place my lips to his.

"I missed you last night," he says against my lips, making me smile and causing my heart to beat that little bit faster.

"Ugh, get a room," I hear a familiar voice shout from behind me. Taylor and I break apart and when I turn I see a smiling Molly with Lois attached to her hip. "I know it took you guys long enough to figure this all out," she says gesturing between us, "but Beth is starting to hyperventilate about the lack of photographer upstairs."

"We're on it," I say as I start pulling Taylor in the direction of the elevators. He pauses briefly to say hello to Molly but in seconds we are heading to the top floor of the hotel to hopefully make Beth's day. As for Mum, well we're about to see how this is going to go down.

"Caleb, about time. Where is this photographer you promised?" Mum barks the second I walk into the room.

"He's here," I say, stepping aside to reveal Taylor behind me.

"What's *he* doing here? I thought you said he wasn't coming."

"Mum," both Beth and I snap at the same time at her attitude.

"He's a photographer, Mum. And a bloody good one." At that announcement Beth is out of her chair, much to the hair stylists annoyance, and launches herself at Taylor. They've met a few times before and although she never said anything I'm pretty sure she was well aware of my feelings for him.

"Thank you so much. You have no idea how much I appreciate you being here." Once Beth's let go of Taylor she turns to me. "You're a little bit awesome, you know that right?" I shrug my shoulders at her in response. "I'm glad you're here, Taylor," she says as she walks away. "And not just as the photographer. Mum..." she prompts as she walks past her.

"Thank you, Taylor," Mum adds, just about managing to crack a smile.

The ceremony is short and sweet. I'd love to be able to say what actually happened but I spent the entire time staring at Taylor's ass. Those trousers just hug it in the most incredible way. I am dying to get them off him. I can see he's more stressed than usual and I can only presume that's because of his mum. We haven't had any time to talk since he arrived and it's killing me that he's so close.

The whole day goes by in a blur of wedding formalities, amazing French food and even better French wine. I get a few fleeting moments with Taylor but nothing like I want.

"Hey, Mum. Having a good day?" I ask when I see her sat alone for the first time all day at the bar.

"Yes. Just look how happy they are," she says with wet eyes as she glances over at Beth and Daniel who are talking to Steven, Daniel's brother, and his wife. "All I want is for my kids to be happy. Find someone they love and spend their lives with them." I look back at her then down at her empty glass wondering how much she's had. "I'm so sorry, Caleb. I'm embarrassed of how I've acted, how selfish I've been. I've been watching you today and it's clear as day how happy Taylor makes you. You obviously do the same for him as well. Not everyone would have hopped on the first plane to be here at the last minute today, especially with how I treated him last time I saw him."

"He's special, Mum."

"I can see that. He was showing me some of the photos he's taken. They are beautiful." I feel myself swell with pride for my man. "I think this all worked out as it should, don't you?" At that moment I feel heat behind me. Mum looks over my shoulder and smiles before getting up off the bar stool and walking away with a smile on her face.

A large pair of hands land on my shoulders and spin me around.

"Hey."

"Hey. How did you do it?"

"Do what?"

"Win my mum around?"

"It wasn't hard. I mean, I'm awesome so it was inevitable it was going to happen eventually," he says with a cocky smile on his face.

"You're a nightmare," I say as I slap his shoulder.

"I'm your nightmare."

Chapter 6

Taylor

"Alright, alright, break it up you two. Grandma's eyes are about to pop out of her head and I need my photographer back," Beth says, making me pull away from Caleb's lips.

I look over her shoulder to see her Grandma grinning at us. It seems she was enjoying the show. "I don't think she has an issue, look at that gleam in her eye."

"Ugh, Taylor," Beth complains but smiles and grabs my hand at the same time. "It's time for our first dance, come on." I put down the drink I've had about two sips of before following behind her like I have all day. And just like I have all day I feel Caleb's eyes burn into the back of me. I swear he didn't watch a second of his sister getting married earlier. Every time I looked back his eyes were glued to my arse, not that I'm complaining. It's nice to know that he's so into me that even his sister tying the knot can't distract him.

When I turned up earlier and found him in his slim fit suit I was taken right back to the first time I laid my eyes on him at Molly's party. He looked just as breathtaking today as he did that night. I'd been on edge since hanging up the phone earlier. What I nearly said out loud to him shook me. The words almost flowed from my lips so easily. I've never said those words out loud to anyone other than my mum and Lilly and the meaning was very different. Does the fact that the words practically fell out of my mouth mean they're true? Am I in love with Caleb West?

The rest of the weekend in Paris is incredible. I've never had the opportunity to travel much outside of the UK. I've only actually flown once before and that was with Lilly a couple of years ago for a week in the sun. It if wasn't for that I wouldn't have had a passport and I wouldn't have got here. I can't lie, attempting to find my way around Heathrow airport alone was a bit of a challenge but knowing who was waiting for me at the other end of the short flight was enough to keep me going.

Caleb and I spend the weekend seeing the sights Paris has to offer. I'm thrilled that it's also his first time here, it meant we could discover everything together. The city is exactly as I expected it to be and I'm gutted that the time comes for us to leave our hotel for the airport. I could easily spend the whole week here.

"Have you got everything?" Caleb asks as he wheels his case to the door.

I look around our room to check I've not left anything behind before taking one last look at the amazing view. I let out a huge breath as I turn to head for the door. I'm really not ready to leave our little paradise yet.

"Yeah, I'm good. When we get back can we book a holiday? Just us two, I don't care where. I want to discover new places like we have here, make some memories together." I don't add that I have so many bad memories from my childhood that I'm hoping the new ones with him will push them out.

"Sounds like a plan. Come on, let's go."

Hand in hand we head down to the hotel reception to say goodbye to Beth and Daniel who are staying here a few more days before heading off on their six-week honeymoon tour around Europe. I've never really spent much time thinking about travelling before but having had a taste of Paris I'm seriously jealous of what they are about to embark on.

I give Beth a kiss on the cheek and shake Daniel's hand before standing back to allow Caleb to have some time with his sister. As we stand there his parents come to join us along with Molly, Ryan and Lois. Last to appear are Steven and his family and once we've all said goodbye to the happy couple we jump in taxis and head for the airport.

"Would you like a drink, sir?" the flight attendant asks once the seat belt sign is off.

"I'm fine, thank you," I answer sadly. I look to my right to see a random stranger sat there. My last minute booking on this flight meant I had to sit away from the others. After being with Caleb almost 24/7 over the past couple of days the separation has hit me kinda hard. Harder than I was expecting it to anyway.

I find the others in baggage reclaim. I came with hand luggage—it wasn't like I had time to pack anything. It's Penny who sees me first and I'm amazed by the smile she gives me when our eyes meet. It seems that saving the day by appearing with my camera has softened her somewhat.

"How was your flight?" she asks when I get close enough to hear her. Anyone eavesdropping would think we were on different flights.

"Long," I reply, even though the flight wasn't much more than an hour, "and lonely," I add.

"Well you're back with us now."

Caleb turns toward us after grabbing a bag off the conveyor belt and his face lights up.

"Hey, we tried waiting for you when we got inside but the attendant moved us on," he says as he runs his hand down my arm. Just that small gesture has goosebumps pricking my skin.

"No worries. Are you all set?" I ask, looking at the pile of cases around his feet.

After stopping for lunch Caleb's parents, Molly, Ryan and Lois all head toward Oxford. Apparently Beth sent a load of stuff back with Penny and Simon so they're dropping it off there before heading back up to Liverpool tomorrow.

"I told you she'd warm to you eventually," Caleb comments as we watch them all walk away. He's right because I just got a pretty big hug off his mum. Something I never thought would happen after that first time I met her.

"Come on, let's go home."

"About that..."

"You kicking me out?"

"No... I was... uh... wondering... wanna move into my room?" Caleb asks in a rush.

A smile breaks across my face. It would be impossible if I wanted to try to play it cool right now because I have no control over my joy.

"You're asking me to move in with you?"

"Yep," he confirms.

"Fucking right I will," I announce before dropping my case and pulling him so we're chest to chest. The kiss I give him is entirely too inappropriate to be happening in the middle of an airport but I couldn't care less. After two and a bit years of trying to break him down, I've finally done it. I knew he wanted me all along.

I'm flying high all the way back to our flat. My smile hasn't faltered, much to Caleb's amusement. Unfortunately though everything comes crashing down very fast when we look up to our front door.

Our usual sleek black shiny door with chrome fittings is now boarded up with some police tape strapped across it.

"What the fuck?" we both ask in unison before rushing forward.

I don't wait for any instruction or even think of any consequences as I launch myself at the wood covering our door.

The force of my body smashes through it easily and I get a look at what is beyond.

"Fuck," is all I can say as I look at our trashed apartment. Everything's either smashed, ripped apart or turned over.

"Fuck," gets repeated behind me as Caleb gets his first look at all his stuff. I may call it our flat but in reality everything in here is his. I just help pay the rent.

We both walk into the room and silently take in the devastation before us.

"You're back," I hear someone say from the doorway. When I turn around I see it's our neighbour. "We tried to get hold of you both but neither of your phones were on."

"We were at a wedding in Paris," I say when it becomes clear that Caleb isn't going to respond. "What happened?"

"No idea. I came back in yesterday evening and saw that your door was swinging on its hinges. I called the police, they sorted this out," he says gesturing toward the boarded up door, "But they really need to speak to you both. They said they didn't think anything was missing. The obvious things like your TV and computer are still here, a little worse for wear mind you." I look over at where the fifty-inch TV usually sits to see it all bent and buckled on the floor.

"Who the fuck?" Caleb mutters quietly to himself as he looks at all his stuff.

A face pops into my head.

"MOTHERFUCKER!"

I pull my phone from my pocket and power it up, or at least I try but it's fucking dead. After rummaging through my case I find the charger and plug it into the wall. After a few seconds it starts up and I scroll through my contacts until I find the number for the phone I gave my mum.

It doesn't ring. It goes straight to voicemail.

"FUCK," I shout again, just about resisting the urge to launch my phone across the room. It's already broken enough from the last time I tried that. "I'm so sorry," I say sadly to Caleb who is looking at me blankly.

"It's not your fault," he says reassuringly.

"It is though. It's fucking *him,* I know it is. I brought this to you." I rub my hands over my short hair before running them down my face.

I take a step back until my arse hits the wall. I lower down and put my head in my hands. Caleb decides that he wants me and this is what I give him. He doesn't deserve this, he's too good for me. I'm a walking fucking disaster.

"Here," our neighbour says, reminding me that we've got an audience. "The coppers said for you to call this number when you returned."

I watch as he backs out of the flat leaving us alone.

"I'm sorry," I repeat.

Caleb walks over to me before lowering down on to his haunches. "Stop that, it's not your fault."

"Yes it is. If it wasn't for me and my fucked-up family this wouldn't be happening."

"Stop it," he snaps, his anger surfacing. "If it was *him* then his actions are nothing to do with you."

"But Mum—"

"You were doing what you thought was best.

Everyone would have done the same thing in your position."

I look up at him sadly.

"Caleb?"

"Yeah?"

"I think I've fallen in love with you."

It's clear from the look on his face that he wasn't expecting that.

"I—" he starts but I cut him off. I'm not finished.

"But if you don't want me and everything that comes with me," I say, gesturing to the devastation around us, "then you need to tell me now because if this goes on any longer I won't be able to walk away from you." The final part of my statement comes out muffled because Caleb gently places his hand over my mouth.

"Shut up, you idiot," he says, dropping forward onto his knees and replacing his hand with his lips.

When he pulls back his eyes are dark and his chest is heaving up and down with his increased breaths. He opens his mouth to say something but we get interrupted.

"Ah you're back. We were just popping in to check on the place."

When I look up I see two policemen standing looking down on us.

They stay for about an hour questioning us and going through everything. I tell them all about my suspicions that it was my stepdad and they say they'll try to pick him up.

Once they've gone we phone a locksmith and attempt to sort through the flat and write an inventory of what is damaged and completely fucked for the insurance company.

It's well after midnight before we call it a day, or night. Caleb ordered us Thai takeout and we sit and eat it out of the tubs on our living room floor seeing as the sofa cushions have been shredded and had all the stuffing pulled out of them.

We may be surrounded by chaos but there's something so calming in this moment. I look up to Caleb to find him already looking over at me. He has a small smile on his face and a glint in his eye.

"I got interrupted earlier," he says, placing his now empty tub down on the floor and turning to look at me. "But what I was going to say was that I think I've been falling in love with you for a long time now. I was just too pig-headed and stubborn to admit it."

My heart thuds in my chest threatening to escape. "Please say that again. I just need to make sure I heard correctly."

Caleb's smile widens as he throws his leg over me so he's straddling me. "I," he says, leaning forward and placing a simple kiss to my lips. "Love." He kisses me again. "You." I don't give him a chance to kiss me this time because I grab on to him and flip him onto his back. I settle myself between his legs, lean forward and kiss him. Here, surrounded by this disaster I kiss him like it's the first and last time I'll ever get the chance. Smashed up flats, fucked-up family, hell, the fucking world is forgotten in those minutes as I try to show him just how much I meant those words earlier. Because I do, more than anything. I may not have much to offer him but love is something I definitely do have. And right there on our living room floor I set about showing him properly.

"I've never made love to anyone before," I admit while running my fingertips over his chest and stomach.

"Me either, it was nice."

"It was nice?" I ask totally affronted by his comment.

"Yeah, nice." He rolls over onto his side and looks at me, he can't contain it though and bursts out laughing. "Your face! It was incredible, Tay." He stretches up and gives me a kiss. "Stop pouting, I said it was incredible. Give me your lips."

He pulls back after a few seconds, his eyebrows are drawn together deep in thought. "I've been thinking, how about we find somewhere new to live?"

"But you love this place."

"Yeah but it's mine. I want something we choose together. Plus, it's never going to be the same now." I instantly go to apologise again but he won't have it.

I call work first thing the next morning, explain what's happened and tell them I'll be back in a few days. Thankfully Paul tells me to take as much time as I need. I don't intend on taking the piss but there are a few things I need to sort out. Mum being one of them.

I discover that the hotel key card that I'd left on my bedside table for her room has disappeared. Giving even more evidence that it was my stepdad.

"Good morning, sir, how can I help?" the lady on reception says when I approach.

"Hi, yeah, there was a Mrs. Bentley-Cox staying in room 304. Could you tell me if she has checked out please?"

"I'm sorry, sir. I can't give details about our guests."

"I booked the room, look at the details. She's my mum and I need to know if she's gone or not."

"Sir—"

"Please." I must look pathetic enough that she caves and tells me that Mum checked out of her room yesterday morning. Just as I suspected.

"Oh hang on, sir," the receptionist says as I turn away. "There's a note to say she left something here for you."

Turning back around I see her rooting through a drawer. "Here."

I take the small piece of paper from her outstretched hand and after thanking her I march from the hotel.

I find a bench a little down the street. I sit and stare at the piece of paper for a few seconds, trying to imagine what could possibly be on it. I come to a conclusion it can only be one thing. And when I open it I find that I'm right.

I'm sorry. x

"Motherfucker," I mutter under my breath and screw the paper up into my palm. That is it. That was her last chance. I warned her and I meant it. I will not help her try to get away from him again.

When I get back to the flat later that afternoon Caleb is just lowering his phone from his ear. His face shows that he hasn't just received good news.

"That was the police," he says sadly.

"Go on."

"They picked up your stepdad earlier. Questioned him."

"And..."

"They can't charge him."

"Why the fuck not?"

"He's got an alibi."

"Of course he fucking has," I mutter as I come to stand in front of our kitchen worktop. I place my palms on the counter and hang my head. "She's never going to leave him is she?"

"Taylor," Caleb says, coming to stand next to me before wrapping me in his arms.

Caleb

"This is the one," Taylor announces as he spins around looking at everything this flat has to offer.

In the past two weeks we have looked at hundreds of apartments online and viewed a handful, none of which have been suitable. The second we were shown the details for this one though, we both knew. This was the one. It's a stunning top floor maisonette of a recently converted warehouse. It's slightly more out of town than our old place but the compromise is so worth it. The space we get for our money is insane. So what, we'll have to spend a little longer each day commuting into the city?

I continue watching Taylor take in all the details. I don't need to see any more. The photos we've seen and his reaction now is all I need. He's looking at the modern kitchen stood in a pool of light that the giant windows let it. One wall is completely glass, giving us an amazing view. Most of the walls are exposed brickwork and the floor is stunningly refurbished dark wood. The mix of both wood and metal throughout this place is incredible. Taylor's boss came up trumps with the estate agent's recommendation. Brian was the only agent to know this was coming on the market and we have been lucky enough to be the first and hopefully only people to view it.

"Where do we sign?" I ask Brian, ripping my eyes away from Taylor's ass as he starts climbing the stairs to check out the bedrooms and bathroom.

"Don't you want to look upstairs?"

"I will but I don't need to. This is our new home," I state proudly.

We spend so long in the flat that Brian has to practically drag us out because he has other clients to meet.

"I can't believe that's going to be our new home," Taylor sighs, he's practically bouncing as we head back into the thick of the city. We have one more stop before going for lunch. "Hey, aren't you excited?" he asks when he sees that I'm looking a little less enthusiastic about it than he is.

"Of course I am. I'm just a little nervous about what's next."

"Oh shut up. It's going to be so hot. I'm already hard

just thinking about it," he announces a little too loudly on a busy London sidewalk.

As we get closer to our destination there seems to be more and more people; that could just be my imagination —or fear—mind you.

"Fuck, that is seriously hot," Taylor says beside me as the heads in front of us part slightly allowing my first glimpse.

There staring back it me in the middle of the city is a fucking giant billboard advertising a brand of underwear that I'm fairly familiar with. Mainly because I'm the one wearing them. There for the world and their wife to see is a fuck knows how many foot billboard of my scantily clad body.

"Please can we get a copy for the wall of our new place?" Taylor asks excitedly. Unfortunately I don't get to answer because his question is overheard by some young women in front of us. I watch in amazement as they look from me to the billboard and back again with their mouths open and their eyes almost popping out of their heads.

The next hour is a blur of excitement and autographs. Yes I actually signed autographs. It was fucking crazy. And I'm not just talking autographs on paper either because I actually signed some woman's boobs. I've never touched a pair of tits in my life before today. I guess it's something I can now tick off my bucket list.

The whole time Taylor stands just to my side with the proudest fucking smirk on his face that I've ever seen.

Once all the crazy has died down a bit I turn to him and wrap my arms around his waist.

"I'm so proud of you," he says, looking down at me.

"Why? I didn't do anything."

"There aren't many people who would look good blown up to forty feet wearing only their underwear."

"You'd look good."

"Obviously," he says with a laugh and I can't help but laugh along with him.

"This is a new start. For both of us." My statement makes him think about everything that's happened and I lose him for a few minutes. "You don't need them," I whisper in his ear. "You've got me. You've got Lilly. Family doesn't have to be by blood, Tay. It can be whoever we want it to be. One day you can get rid of them completely maybe and change your name to West. I think Taylor West has quite a ring to it, don't you?"

When his eyes come back to mine they are a little wet. I love it when he allows me to see a chink in the rock hard exterior. It makes me fall for him that little bit more than I already have.

I watch as he squares his shoulders and thinks about what I said.

"New start," he says with a head nod. "Shall we start it with Chinese or sushi?"

"Sushi."

With one last look at my giant body, and one final photograph of it on Taylor's phone, hand in hand we walk to start the next chapter of our lives. Together.

Epilogue

Taylor

"Hey, you made it," Lilly says, stating the obvious the second she pulls the front door open.

"Of course." I wrap her in a tight hug.

The last time I was stood on her doorstep I was a broken man. This time though I feel better than I've ever done.

"Caleb," she greets and I step aside so she can hug him too.

We both drop our bags in the hallway and follow her to the living room.

"Fuck, look at those two go!" I say as two small people start dragging their bodies over toward us doing a great snake/seal impression. I crouch down and grab one under each arm before I start spinning them around the room.

"Taylor," Lilly screeches, "they've just eaten."

I continue for a few more seconds just for my own amusement so I can watch her panic.

Once she's happy they're not about to puke everywhere she leaves to get us both drinks. Both Nathan and Natalie take one look at me and make a beeline for my feet. Leaning down I grab them again, sit one on each leg and start making silly faces at them. They both giggle in the most infectious way.

I look up when I feel Caleb's stare burning into me. He has the sappiest look on his face.

"What?"

"You're so good with them."

"What these two? How could you not be? They're adorable."

"Do you want kids?"

"It's not something I've ever really put much thought into. I was convinced I didn't want a relationship so kids were never really in the picture."

"And what about now you're in a relationship?"

"I think anything is a possibility."

Our conversation gets cut short when Lilly reappears with two beers.

"So where's the birthday boy?" I ask, referring to the reason we're here. Lucas hit the big 30 yesterday so Lilly invited us for the weekend along with Marcus, Lucas's brother, and a couple of friends to celebrate.

"He's gone to the hotel to pick up Marcus, Imogen and Eve. Joe and Nat are upstairs getting changed and I think Dec's on his way.

Two hours later, the twins are in bed and the party has really started. By that I mean CBeebies has been turned off, the mountain of toys have been cleared away and the takeaway has arrived. It's not exactly the kind of partying that I'm used to but I couldn't think of a better way to spend my Friday night than with the people I love the most.

"What did you think of that sofa I sent you a picture of?" Lilly asks after a mouth full of chicken korma. Fucking lightweight with her pussy curry!

"Loved it. We ordered it that night. We're still looking for the right bedroom furniture though so keep looking."

I swear Lilly almost had an orgasm when I sent her pictures of our new flat. The noises she was making over the phone while she looked at them were pretty obscene. She's been sending us images of all sorts of furniture, curtains and knick-knacks everyday since. Most of which we've ordered straight away.

We continue chatting away until the doorbell rings. It's clear from the silent conversation that Lilly and Lucas have between them that they're not expecting anyone and don't know who it is.

Lilly gets up and disappears leaving us all to wonder.

"OH MY GOD!" is squealed from the front door making us all look up and for Lucas to get to his feet. He's just about to march toward the noise when Lilly follows it up with "NICOLE!"

The next few minutes are a blur because no sooner have we all continued eating does a brown ball of fluff come bounding into the room. I don't realise it's there until it launches itself on my lap, squeezing its way between me and the table so it can lick up the remains of my lamb madras.

"What the fuck?" I shout trying to grab the fluffy thing and move it away from what it definitely should not be eating. I feel sorry for whoever is at the wrong end of that tomorrow.

I just about get him to the ground before Lilly comes in followed by Nicole. I've met her a couple of times but I hardly recognise her. Her skin is pale, her eyes are dark and sunken and her usually gorgeous thick hair is limp and straggly around her shoulders.

"Everyone, this is Nicole, my best friend. Nicole, this is everyone." Lilly goes around the table to introduce Nicole to those who haven't met her before. It's not until she gets halfway around the table that we all notice something is missing. Or should I say someone.

"Where's Dec gone?"

Find out what's going on with Nicole and Declan in Falling For Declan!
ONE-CLICK NOW

READ FALLING FOR DANIEL FOR FREE!

Grab your FREE copy of Falling For Daniel now:

Click here to claim your copy

ACKNOWLEDGMENTS

I can't lie, I felt a bit of pressure after Lilly and Lucas's story. The reviews and messages I received blew me away so I needed to make sure Taylor didn't disappoint.

I hope you enjoyed finding out a little more about the mystery that was Taylor. I have to admit I have a bit of a sweet spot for him and Caleb, and I enjoyed writing their hot little story.

Thank you to everyone who is reading this and still on this crazy journey with me. I'm getting toward the end of this series and I'm not sure how I feel about saying goodbye to all these characters, they've become quite a big part of my life. That being said though I've got some exciting things planned for the coming months that I'm excited to share with you all.

I want to say a huge thank you to Deanna, Helen, Michelle and Tracy for beta reading Taylor for me. You all put my mind to rest with your love for these two.

Nicole, as always, for your advice and support, it really is priceless. I wouldn't be where I am now without you.

Evelyn at Pinpoint Editing, thank you for working your magic on Taylor like you have all the others.

Colleen and Itsy Bitsy Book Bits, again you guys have been incredible. I love working with you all.

Thank you to all the bloggers who have shared for me, without you guys no one would know my books are out there so thank you for spreading the word.

Finally Deanna, I've dedicated this one to you because of everything you do for me. You spend time every day helping me out and I seriously can't thank you enough. I'm so excited to be working with you on our new blog—Laid-back Book Bitches if you don't already like us! I feel like it's the start of something amazing, I can't wait to see where it takes us.

Nicole and Declan's story is up next, and I can't tell you how excited I am to write it. It's been bouncing around in the head for over two years now and I am itching to get it out and to find out more about both of them.

ABOUT THE AUTHOR

Tracy Lorraine is a *USA Today* and *Wall Street Journal* bestselling new adult and contemporary romance author. Tracy has recently turned thirty and lives in a cute Cotswold village in England with her husband, baby girl and lovable but slightly crazy dog. Having always been a bookaholic with her head stuck in her Kindle, Tracy decided to try her hand at a story idea she dreamt up and hasn't looked back since.

Be the first to find out about new releases and offers. Sign up to my newsletter here.

If you want to know what I'm up to and see teasers and snippets of what I'm working on, then you need to be in my Facebook group. Join Tracy's Angels here.

Keep up to date with Tracy's books at
www.tracylorraine.com

ALSO BY TRACY LORRAINE

Buy your next paperback personalised by me!

www.tracylorraine.com

Falling Series

Falling for Ryan: Part One #1

Falling for Ryan: Part Two #2

Falling for Jax #3

Falling for Daniel (A Falling Series Novella)

Falling for Ruben #4

Falling for Fin #5

Falling for Lucas #6

Falling for Caleb #7

Falling for Declan #8

Falling For Liam #9

Printed in Great Britain
by Amazon

46058786R00071